Praise for

ENTANGLED THORNS

by

Melinda Clayton

Entangled Thorns weaves a compelling tale of family dysfunction and healing; many can relate to this story, a multi-generational saga of life in Appalachia in the recent past, and many could testify to these same emotions which run rampant in their own families.

Robin Tidwell, All on the Same Page Bookstore, Creve Coeur, Missouri

In my review of Melinda Clayton's book *Appalachian Justice*, I compared her writing to the great Flannery O'Connor. If Flannery were alive today, she'd no doubt be reading Clayton's latest book called *Entangled Thorns* and singing its praises.

Shannon L. Yarbrough, Vine Voice

ENTANGLED THORNS

Cedar Hollow Series, Book 3

by

Melinda Clayton

Thomas-Jacob Publishing, LLC
USA

ENTANGLED THORNS

by Melinda Clayton

Published by: Thomas-Jacob Publishing, LLC
ThomasJacobPublishing@gmail.com

Cover Art: Clarissa Yeo, Book Cover Art:
http://www.bookcoversale.com/#

Library of Congress Control Number: 2019942531
1. Fiction/psychological suspense 2. Fiction/small town and rural
ISBN-13: 978-0-9895729-2-7
ISBN-10: 0-9895729-2-7
Thomas-Jacob Publishing, LLC Deltona, Florida, USA

Third Edition
First Printing: July 2013

Dedication

To my husband, Donny, and my children, Caleb and Isaac. In the words of Kay Langley, "Some people, like me, are blessed with a good family all the way around."

Acknowledgements

A special thank you to the Wednesday Night Book Lovers of Deltona, with a shout out to Patti Lapinsky, Pamela Eifert, Karen Hook, and Diane Mastrangelo-Rohmeyer, my last- minute beta-readers. Thank you, ladies!

A heartfelt thank you to my parents, as well, who have made this such an enjoyable journey.

For entangled like thorns, and drunken as with their drink, they are consumed utterly like dry stubble.

~ Nahum 1:10

Chapter 1

Beth Pritchett Sloan

The sun fades away in the west, and I pour myself a second glass of chardonnay, a pricier selection than my typical fare. We generally save the good stuff for company, but it's been a particularly trying day. The decanter is slick with sweat, the chill long since faded. This does not bother me. As quickly as I'll be emptying the bottle, it's hardly worth rousing to trek to the refrigerator between glasses, and I long ago gave up the pretension of an ice bucket. I'll drink it warm.

Given long enough, I might even omit the goblet. I've not previously sunk to that level of intemperance, but the swift road to my decline has left me uncertain as to what my final destination might be. The image of me imbibing straight from the source no longer seems beyond the realm of possibility, though I'm not quite there yet.

Replacing the bottle on the marbled windowsill with a satisfying *thunk*, I settle back into my overstuffed chair. It isn't a comfortable seat, chosen more for looks than functionality, the upholstery scratchy and unyielding, bought in a moment of presumption. But it's the only one that affords me the view I want. I have to crane my neck to the left and peer between the sprawling houses across the street, but if I angle my head just so, I can get a glimpse of the western sky.

Vaguely, I wonder when the sunsets became so subdued. Dull pink, dirty yellow, in the distance the colors are smeared across the dingy Memphis sky like a vapid stain, and I have a fleeting memory of tattered clothing hanging from a line, blowing in the wind. The air is wet and heavy, dripping with the stifling humidity that rolls across town from the muddy waters of the Mississippi River. The window fogs in front of me, the droplets creating rivulets on the steamy glass. In my current state of mind, the whole world appears to be weeping.

The flaming sunsets of my childhood had stretched across the West Virginia mountaintops as if painted by God himself, the hellfire and brimstone God I heard Brother Thomas Hudson, Jr. preach about down at the Cedar Hollow Baptist Church on the rare occasions my family occupied a pew. As a child, I took it literally when Brother Hudson spoke about his personal relationship with God. Observing the preacher's deep creases and lines, I had assumed he and God were roughly the same age, though in retrospect the poor man was probably no older than I am now.

As I tilt my head, savoring the taste of expensive wine as it slides down my throat, I'm amused at the memory of my childish interpretations. I haven't thought of Brother Hudson in years, and for a fleeting instant I wonder if he's still there, perched behind the pulpit, fist waving in indignation at the sinful nature of his parishioners. Of course he's not; he'd be long dead by now. I swallow, leaning my head back against the rough upholstery, too disappointed in the faded sunset to risk the crick in my neck I'm sure to receive by seeking it out.

There are a few things I miss from my childhood, and the sunsets are one of them. My family, however, is not. The letter in my lap lays like a weight across my thighs, pinning me down and holding me prisoner, wiping out any comfort I might have found from the wine. With the exception of my sister, I haven't seen my family of origin in nearly twenty-seven years, not since Luke died. And now this.

The house is quiet, and my thoughts seem to echo not only through my own mind, but through the darkened rooms. I am alone here, literally as well as figuratively. Mark is still at work, or wherever he is when he isn't home, possibly with a patient or answering an emergency call, or—the nagging thought won't leave me alone—maybe having an affair with his voluptuous new receptionist. I'm too old and tired to entertain the thought of competing with her salacious seduction. I would like to believe our years together, our children, and the home we've created would outweigh whatever attraction Mark might feel for her, but I don't know, and at this point it hardly matters. It's too late.

My older child, Matthew, recently moved into the dorms of the University of Tennessee. I smile at the thought of my quiet, serious son. Matthew wants to follow in his father's footsteps, entering into the university's pre-med program with a full course load. He's an earnest young man, very much like his father was when we met. I only hope Matthew won't learn to wield that earnestness like a sword the way his father does. But I'm not being fair; it isn't Mark's fault I can't live up to his expectations.

Unlike Matthew, Marissa is anything but serious. Irreverent, raucous, Marissa has been a challenge since the day she was born. I congratulate myself on getting her through her first seventeen years of life relatively intact. I only hope I can get her through her last year of high school before she completely rebels against my authority.

Marissa stormed out hours ago, after another of our battles, texting me later to let me know she was with friends at the mall. That text gives me hope. Marissa is a good daughter, a sweet girl in spite of our skirmishes, but I can feel her slipping away. Always headstrong, her sudden temper flares have become more frequent and longer lasting. I'm not sure the cause, and I don't know how to fix it, but her temperament is all too familiar. This tortures me. I love my daughter. I don't want to lose her, too.

I swish the drink around in my glass again, watching as the liquid sparkles in the light from the lamp by my side. More often than not, I spend my evenings sitting alone in the lamplight. I ignore the phone calls confirming church bake sales and band booster events; I disregard the doorbell, turning away impromptu invitations to share gossip and drinks on someone's back deck.

When the children were younger, evening was my favorite time of day, regardless of the season. I loved the softening around the edges, the muted light, the gentle breeze that always seemed to pick up just as the sun slipped toward the horizon. I was comforted by the sight of cars turning into carports up and down the street as families reunited.

In warmer weather, we gathered outside as soon as the dinner dishes were cleared, as if summoned by some sort of unspoken communication. The parents and the children, at first in our own yards and driveways, eventually drawn together, sometimes content to stand on sidewalks, other times settling on lounge chairs and deck swings, the location unimportant, the company everything. Neckties were loosened, high heels were kicked off, and drinks were poured as the children played around us, two on bikes, another three on a swing set, a passel playing hide and seek through the adjoining yards.

I still hear the sounds, the deep rumble of a man's laugh, the higher melody of women's voices, shrieks of children at play. They resonate, muffled through my window, but I no longer join in. Instead, I sit alone with my thoughts. On clear evenings I watch the sunset before pulling the shades, complete in my isolation. Sometimes I ruminate on those early days, when things were different. I remember children running through the house, laughter bouncing off the walls, wrestling sleeping bags down from the linen closet for another slumber party.

I remember standing over the stove, timing the meatloaf just right so that after an exhausting day of building up his medical practice, Mark would enter into a home warm with family and food, the table set, the platters steaming. I remember that for a little while, a moment in time so brief I can barely grasp it before it dissipates like a fine mist, I was the perfect wife and mother, our home the epitome of domestic bliss. As pathetic as it may seem, these solitary evenings with my memories are now the highlight of my life.

I have enough insight to realize I've created the circumstances that sadden me, but not enough to know how it could have turned out any differently. My family of origin was not an easy one. My grandfather, Lucas Pritchett, Sr.—known as Old Man Pritchett to the good folks of Cedar Hollow, West Virginia, and as Papaw Pritchett to us—was a smalltime moonshiner and bootlegger, making 'shine in the stills behind the rundown shack he called home, and running it through Mingo County back when no stranger in his right mind would dare to drive through Williamson after sunset.

Mingo County was pieced together out of parts of Logan County back in 1895, in an attempt to get a better handle on the moonshine activity in the area. Williamson, the county seat, is a pretty little town today, rich with West Virginia history. But in Papaw Pritchett's day many claimed, and I believe them, that Mingo County was built by, run by, and governed by bootleggers, some in overalls like my grandfather, and some, they said, wearing the uniform of the law.

I suppose my grandfather's claim to fame, if there is one, was that he helped build Mingo. To this day his body is no doubt buried somewhere within the county lines; it was never found, but it was on the night of one such run that Papaw Pritchett failed to make it home. It wasn't entirely unexpected; bootlegging was an ugly business back then. I imagine it still is, whether it's whiskey or meth, the modern-day equivalent. At any rate, Papaw Pritchett wasn't missed. Outside of making and running hooch, which most of my family knew how to do, he'd been a regular bastard.

The educated people with whom I'm acquainted laugh when I mention my family history. To them, it's quaint, a small slice of Americana that no longer exists. But it does still exist; I know this because many of my family members still live it. Oh, they don't run 'shine across county lines anymore, but I'd be willing to bet my cellar full of fine wines they continue to make it for themselves, and no doubt bootleg it to any tightlipped locals who crave the taste.

Papaw Pritchett's son, my father, was known simply as Junior. I suppose we must have called him dad, but I don't remember calling him anything at all. I don't remember ever addressing him, except in answer to his orders. I knew him primarily as, "Yes, sir."

When Papaw didn't come home, my father took over the running of the stills. He was, after all, the oldest of the ten children, and therefore the most experienced with the process. If Papaw Pritchett's whiskey running business was smalltime, my father's was miniscule, not because he couldn't make decent rotgut—his was known as some of the best around due to the amount of cane sugar mixed into the mash, a recipe he proudly referred to as *pure 'shine*—but because in the absence of Papaw Pritchett's iron will, my family always had a tendency to drink more than they sold.

My job, along with my younger siblings and cousins, was as taster. I don't remember when they first began using me in this manner, but I do remember when they began using Naomi. She had just celebrated her first birthday. I was three at that time, old enough to have learned there was no use fighting it. Naomi, however, fought with every muscle in her tiny little body, screaming until she was blue in the face that first time and many times after.

Naomi was always the stronger of the two of us in spite of my advantage in age. As I think about it, I realize Marissa is very much like Naomi, a fact made more interesting because they've never met. This realization brings with it a pang of regret. As far as I know, Naomi doesn't even know I have children. Although we ran away together, we haven't spoken since before my children were born.

As Naomi would eventually learn, screaming worked against us when we were on the job. The more extreme our reaction to the squeezing forced into our mouths, the better the quality of the 'shine was believed to be. This was apparently a huge source of amusement for the numerous relatives that seemed always to be camped in lean-tos and tents behind our shack. Not surprisingly, it's also the source of the many fillings and crowns that now adorn my teeth. I suppose I should be grateful they never called us in to taste until after the flame test had been conducted. Tasting ruined our teeth, but at least we weren't dead from lead poisoning.

The sun sets and I sit staring out at the darkness watching the street lights switch on, illuminating the Germantown neighborhood that has been my home for the past eighteen years. In Germantown, we like to pretend we're safe from the poverty and crime that exists in our sister city to the west. We trim our hedges and water our lawns and have weekend barbeques and neighborhood watches and pretend not to know what's out there, although just last week three murders occurred within ten miles of my upper-crust neighborhood. Our safe cocoon is just an illusion, and it strikes me as sadly amusing that I've come so far to go nowhere. But how could I have done otherwise? The person I seek to escape is myself.

I lift the bottle, struggling with the cork. As I pour my third glass I promise it will be my last for the night, but I know I'm a liar even as I make the promise. *You need to come home,* the letter says, but there's no point in going home. The past is done; it can't be changed no matter how much we might wish otherwise.

In the early days the wine brought me temporary peace, but that hasn't been the case for a long time. I need to let it go, this habit. The only thing that keeps me from stopping is the fear that I can't. God, I've made a mess of things.

Chapter 2

Naomi Pritchett Wells

"A letter came for you today." That was my assistant, Stephanie. She held a white envelope towards me as I looked up from my desk, confused for a moment. I'd been running through a vast wasteland with vampires hot on my trail, or at least the character in my latest fantasy book had, and it took a moment to reorient myself to my bright, sun-filled Florida room.

"Back on earth yet?" Stephanie asked, smiling. "Sorry for the interruption." Stephanie had been my assistant for the past eight years, since right after the second book in my series had finally hit its mark and I could afford an assistant. I returned the smile.

"It's actually a relief," I answered her. "You and Shiva are much better company than vampires and werewolves." From her cushion on the window seat Shiva opened one eye and stretched, conveying as only a cat can that I wasn't worth her time. "Although," I continued, eying Shiva, "the life forms in the sixth realm are definitely friendlier." I reached for the envelope.

It was a typical number ten, nothing special about it. Except, of course, for the return address. *Mrs. Kay Langley, 102 Foothills Rd., Cedar Hollow, West Virginia.* Kay Langley, the only one from Cedar Hollow who had ever attempted to stay in touch with me. Kay's family owned the diner in the tiny town in which I'd grown up, population, last I'd heard, of two-hundred-twelve. My older sister had waitressed at the diner briefly in her teens. The last letter I'd received from Kay had been just over a year ago, letting me know my father had died. I had not returned for the funeral.

Twenty-seven years ago, shortly after the death of my brother Luke, my older sister Beth and I had taken the early morning train out of Cedar Hollow and we hadn't been back since, nor had we heard from any of our dozens of relatives scattered throughout those mountains in all the intervening years. At least I hadn't. I couldn't speak for Beth, since I also hadn't heard from her in years.

Stephanie still stood in front of my desk, awaiting instruction. "It's a letter from an old family friend," I said. "I haven't heard from her since my father passed away."

Stephanie nodded briefly, a frown of concern creasing her forehead. "Can I get you anything? Something to buffer the blow? Dull the pain? Banish the demons?"

I laughed. "Now see, Steph, that's why you're my assistant. I think I'll pass on the offer, however, since it's only ten in the morning." As Stephanie well knew, I hadn't had a drop of alcohol since I was thirteen, when I'd graduated from taster duty and left the job to Luke and my younger cousins. In my view, particularly given my family history, drinking alcohol was tantamount to a slow, painful suicide. "But I would like some privacy," I said. "Personal demons and family ghosts require it, you know."

Stephanie quietly closed the door behind her, and I ran my nail under the flap of the envelope and removed the folded note inside. I snapped open the cheap paper without hesitation, as if I were ripping off a scab which, figuratively speaking, I knew I might very well be doing. I lay the handwritten note on my desk and pulled the lamp over for a better look, scanning through Kay's spidery scrawl.

When finished, I refolded the letter and put it carefully back into the envelope, securing it behind the box of staples in the right-hand drawer of my antique oak desk. There would be no more writing today, and that irritated me immensely. I stood from behind the desk and walked briskly to the side door that led directly to my husband's home office, entering without knocking.

I couldn't help but smile at Evan as he glanced up at my intrusion. His gray hair was wild about his head and I knew he'd been running his fingers through it in an unconscious gesture of thought. His eyes were wide behind thick glasses, just as mine must have been when Stephanie interrupted me with the mail.

We're very similar, Evan and I. We met in a writing workshop over twenty years ago. Evan is the more talented of the two of us, though he'd say otherwise. He hit the jackpot shortly after we married with his first science fiction work. It had taken me a good twelve years after that before hitting on my own small success.

"Q.'s back," he said, returning my smile.

"Ah. And what helpful advice does she have for you?" Q. Stein was a book reviewer who had followed Evan since the publication of his first book. Caustic, sarcastic, and painfully patronizing, Evan had initially been taken aback by Q. Stein's reviews, but over time had come to appreciate Q.'s approach. Stein was obviously intelligent, often catching mistakes Evan and I, as well as his publisher, had missed. His most recent published novel had been out for over two months without a review from Stein, and Evan had begun to wonder if his loyal critic had finally defected.

"Well," Evan said, "I'm relieved she's—or he's—still here, and even more relieved I got the ellipses right this time, but apparently I have a problem with my setting. Q. says it's Candy Landesque. She says in her review she nearly went into a diabetic coma just from reading. She's really hoping I'll choose another setting before I do irreparable harm to some unsuspecting soul."

"Colorful as always, I see." I settled myself onto the corner of the broad desk.

"I'd be disappointed with anything else," Evan replied, moving a pile of papers aside. "She's really going to hate that I'm writing another in the series."

"But she'll buy it anyway," I said, "if for no other reason than to critique it." I had never been as appreciative of Q.'s reviews as had Evan.

He shrugged. "I've come to depend on her reviews. I'd feel jilted if she left me now." He exited out of the open screen. "How's your morning shaping up? Getting much done?"

"Slow progress," I told him. "The vampires won't cooperate, and I received a letter from an old family friend in Cedar Hollow, which put a considerable damper on things." I waited for his reaction.

"Oh." He sat up straighter, blinking, trying to adjust to the world outside of his computer monitor.

"Kay Langley, from the diner. Remember my stories about Peggy's Diner?"

Evan nodded. "The best key lime pie in West Virginia."

I was touched that he remembered. "Right. Anyway, Kay is asking me to visit my mother."

Evan frowned, scrutinizing my face before responding. "Is your mother ill?"

"Yes and no." I drummed a pencil against the desk, full of nervous energy. "According to Kay, she's lost her mind." I waited for that to sink in. "Kay thinks I should go see her."

He leaned back in his chair with his fingers laced behind his head, a position I knew to be his *critical analysis* position. "That's what Kay thinks, but I'm more interested in what you think. What do you want to do, Naomi?"

One of the many things I love about Evan is that he accepts me without question. No lectures about how I should make peace with my mother, no remonstrations about wasted opportunities or lifelong regrets. Evan's first concern is that I make decisions that lead to my own sense of health and well-being. He also knows that for the majority of my life, that has meant estrangement from my family. Or at least that's what I had always believed. For whatever reason, Kay's letter was stirring up doubts.

When I thought about his question, I knew exactly what I wanted to do. "I want to talk to my sister," I told him.

"Then give her a call," he said, spreading his arms wide, as if the answer were obvious.

I was surprised after all the time that had passed, it really was that simple. Somehow I hadn't thought it would be.

Chapter 3

Kay Langley

When for generations your family has owned the only diner within fifty miles of town, you know things. My granddaddy built Peggy's Diner smack-dab in the middle of Cedar Hollow, West Virginia, way back in 1908 and named it after his only surviving baby. I reckon after losing four babies, three of them boys, he figured he better just be grateful for what he had, so Peggy's Diner it was.

My family has been working this diner ever since. My momma, Peggy, died in '81 at seventy-six years of age after spending nearly all of her life either learning how to run this diner or running it. Momma did such a fine job of running the diner that Daddy retired early from the railroad. He had a good ten years of fishing and hunting and helping Momma before he passed in '74.

Upon Momma's death, the diner fell to me and my brother, but Paul was quick to sell me his share. He hadn't lived in Cedar Hollow since he'd married, and he didn't have plans to return. By that time, Paul was more interested in getting his kids through college than he was in running a diner, so for the next twenty-four years the diner was mine.

I officially retired six years ago after I lost my husband. That's when I turned the diner over to the fourth generation, my son Andrew, but I still work it like nothing ever changed. If I wasn't working I don't know what I'd be doing. Working is living, to me. I found that out real quick after I lost my Howard.

Bless Andrew's heart; he lets me do as much or as little as I feel like doing. Andrew is my baby, the only one of my three children who wanted to stay in Cedar Hollow. I sure am glad he did. I don't know what I'd do without my Andrew, and it looks to be that his daughter Hannah may just be the next in line. I ain't never seen a child with such a good head for business.

As I was saying, when you own a diner it's like you hear all the conversations people would be having at their kitchen tables in their own homes. Sometimes they forget you're there, but sometimes they bring you into the conversation like you're supposed to be a part of it. I reckon there is something about being served good food by good people that makes folks open up more than they might otherwise do.

If a town can have a heart, I expect this diner is it. Everything that goes on in this town ends up being talked about here sooner or later. It was here folks come together to grieve the Wallington Mine explosion of '35. It was here they worried on Billy May Platte's disappearance back in '45, and here again where they gathered to discuss it when she come back to town thirty years later with Roy Campbell's stepdaughter, Jessie, in tow.

My diner is where folks sat and speculated on Roy Campbell, and his buddy Jimmy Williamson, too. Both of them no account thugs had run off and deserted their families back in '75, leaving poor Jessie with no one to care for her. Unlike Billy May, them two never did turn back up, and I expect the town is better for it. I know for a fact Jessie is. As time has passed, the idea of what happened to them men has sort of developed into our own unsolved mystery, though I imagine folks like speculating on it more than they care about trying to solve it.

It was here, too, everyone showed up to celebrate Jessie's first movie, *The Devil's Mine*. Jessie made that movie for Billy May, on account of Billy May taking her in and raising her. It wasn't meant to be a true movie, but we all knew it was based on the Wallington explosion. Billy May was so proud of Jessie and that movie, I'll tell you that. We all was.

Just a few months ago near about the whole town showed up at my diner to discuss what happened up at the children's lodge Jessie built on Crutcher Mountain. Lord, that was a shock, that one was. I'm just glad they got it all sorted out and back on track for the kids.

Since all them shenanigans, Jessie's been spending a whole lot more time here, and that's a good thing. Seems to me, Jessie's realizing she don't like Hollywood quite as much as she used to. There is something to be said for small towns, where you know everybody and everybody is looking out for you.

I apologize for my ramblings; I know I tend to go on, but all of this is to say that any- and everything that goes on in this town eventually gets talked about here in my diner. That's how I come to know about Geraldine Pritchett losing her mind. It was Andrew who told me.

He said last week when the Pritchett boys come in for lunch they was quieter than usual. You can always tell when a Pritchett comes in because they're so blamed loud. Noise just seems to follow the Pritchetts, but that day Andrew said they was so quiet at first he didn't even realize they was there.

Andrew was running the diner alone that day because Riva had the day off and I was having a spell with my back. Being on my feet all these years has taken its toll, I'm sorry to say, and some days the only thing to do is rest the pain with the heating pad. Andrew was in the back on the grill and didn't hear the bell when they come in. Dennis Lane from over at Mr. Smith's General Store was sitting at the counter having lunch with his daddy, Darryl, and he's the one who brought the Pritchett boys to Andrew's attention.

Funny how we all still call them the Pritchett boys. Not a one of Old Man Pritchett's ten kids is under sixty by now. Two of them, Junior and Earl, are already dead, but in a small town once you get stuck with a label there ain't no getting around it, so the Pritchett boys it continues to be.

Well, Andrew went over to see to them and that's when they told him Geraldine had just quit everything. Said it started one day about a month ago when Erma from the boarding home called Wally and said Geraldine wouldn't get out of bed, just plumb refused to get up and wouldn't tell nobody what was wrong. Wally and Wayne went over there to see what Erma was talking about, and Geraldine wouldn't even look at them; Wayne told Andrew she looked right through them like they wasn't even there.

After Junior's death, Geraldine had finally moved out of that raggedy shack on Rugged Creek and taken up a room in Dr. Leary's old house, the one Erma Puckett bought years and years ago and turned into a boarding home, just after Dr. Leary died. Erma had named the place Vines and Roses Boarding Home, but just like the Pritchett boys will always be boys no matter how old they get, the Leary place will always be the Leary place no matter what the sign out front says.

Anyway, Erma and the Pritchett boys tried to coax Geraldine out of bed, helping to prop her up, but she let herself go limp as a flour sack, slipping right out of their hands. They didn't know what to do; they thought maybe if they let her be, she'd come to her senses the next day, but the next day it was even worse. She stopped eating, wouldn't even take a drink of water. Erma called the Pritchett boys again to come and see to Geraldine. Erma does the best she can, but she's getting on up in age, and Geraldine needed more help than Erma could give her.

Junior's brothers carried her out to the truck that morning, and Wally drove while Wayne held onto Geraldine as tight as his crippled hands would let him. Wayne's hands has been scarred for years from what the Pritchetts always claimed was a gasoline explosion. The story they told was Wayne was careless, lighting gasoline to burn off a trash pile, but given what the Pritchetts is known for, I always had my suspicions about that tale. Most of us did, I reckon, but that ain't neither here nor there. Anyway, Wally said if Wayne hadn't been holding onto Geraldine, she would have slid clean down to the floorboard. They drove her to Dr. Landis' office here in town, but he sent them on to Huntington. Said it wasn't a physical thing that ailed her.

Wayne said the fancy doctor in Huntington gave her a whole bunch of pills she refused to take, and got her some kind of caseworker to check in on her, and a Home Health person to make sure she's bathed and fed. But she still ain't talking. Andrew said Wayne told him it's like she just decided to quit living. When Andrew told me that, my chest seized right up, constricting my breath; I can't imagine nothing worse than sitting around waiting to die.

I had seen Geraldine around town several times over the last months, and I'll tell you the truth, it was nice to see her, though she did look awful skinny. We'd been fairly close when we was young, but once she got in with all them Pritchetts they was such a rough crowd I more or less lost touch with Geraldine. Lately I had been thinking about inviting her to the house, but I hadn't gotten around to it yet. I was sorry for that.

Well, after Andrew shared all that with me, I knew what I had to do. I had to send for her girls, Beth and Naomi, although hadn't a one of us seen either one of them in years. Them girls wasn't even grown before they hightailed it out of Cedar Hollow. I couldn't blame them for that. There wasn't nothing for them here. In Cedar Hollow, being a Pritchett has a way of setting a person back in life whether it's deserved or not; the only way to escape that fact is to leave.

I imagine all of us understood their leaving. Some may have even understood why they never did come back to see their momma, not even once, but I wasn't one of them. Funny thing is, it ain't like there was a big fight that caused them girls to stay gone, leastways not one that I know about, and I reckon if it had happened I'd know it. I didn't agree with them girls staying gone from their momma like that, and I wanted to let them know she needed them now.

I hoped they'd come. I imagined they would; it's hard to ignore it when a momma calls, even if that momma don't know she's calling.

Chapter 4

Beth Pritchett Sloan

Marissa is nearly impossible to wake up in the mornings. Even as an infant she slept through the night, hard as that is to believe. She was such an *easy* baby. If only, I often think, I'd known how grateful I should have been during that time. Marissa's later years have been anything but easy. Now that she's a teenager I have to literally pull her out of bed, covers off, lights on, and threats of cold water. And that's only the beginning of our day.

Just after my third attempt to rouse her at nearly eleven o'clock on a sweltering summer morning, with her orthodontist appointment scheduled for less than an hour away, the phone rang. I checked the caller ID but didn't recognize the number. Ordinarily, I'd choose not to answer. I don't know what was different about that call, but for whatever reason, I clicked *on.*

"Hello?"

"Beth?"

It had been more than twenty years since I'd heard that voice, but I recognized it immediately; the Appalachian drawl, softened by the years, was an integral part of who I am. I knew then that she'd also received a letter. My heart stuttered in my chest; I took a moment to collect my thoughts.

"Naomi," I finally said.

"What are you going to do?"

I nearly laughed; Naomi had never been one to beat around the bush. "I'm fine, thanks," I answered the unasked question. "And you?"

Naomi did laugh then, a husky note against my ear. "I'm sorry, Beth, that was terrible of me, wasn't it? Of course I want to know how you are. It's hard to believe it's been so long since we've spoken. You sound exactly the same. I don't even know where to start with my questions, other than the immediate one. Did Kay write to you, too?"

I nodded against the phone. "She did. I got it a couple of days ago. I haven't known what to think of it all. I haven't even mentioned it to Mark yet." There was silence on the other end before I realized she didn't know who I meant. "My husband," I clarified for her. "I haven't told him about it yet."

"Yes, I know," she answered. "You married Dr. Mark Sloan twenty-three years ago. I vaguely remember him as a tall, skinny guy with glasses, very serious. You have two children, Matthew, age nineteen, who is enrolled at the University of Tennessee, and Marissa, seventeen. You live in Germantown, Tennessee. How am I doing so far?"

I was impressed. "You've kept up with me?" I hated the note of pleasure in my voice, not even sure why it should matter after all this time.

"Enough to know the basics," Naomi answered, and then paused. I think both of us were overwhelmed by the reality of our situation. Naomi and I had always been close as girls. We'd shared everything from clothes to a suitcase and a train ride out of town when we'd finally realized we couldn't stay.

We'd landed in Memphis, a destination chosen for no other reason than we both loved the blues, and the tickets were cheap. In the beginning weeks we'd had naïve dreams of singing in one of the bars along Beale Street, ridiculous dreams for girls as young and inexperienced as we were. Luckily those dreams lasted only as long as it took us to wear out our welcome at the Salvation Army shelter on Monroe Avenue.

Eventually we'd found waitressing jobs, lying about our age in order to be allowed to serve beer. Along with two other waitresses whose names I don't even remember, we pooled our money and rented a garage apartment attached to a single-family home in Midtown, just off of Stonewall.

We'd considered ourselves quite stylish back in those days, living in an area that on the best of days seemed young and upwardly mobile, but on the worst seemed a step too close to the shadier side of town just south of Poplar Avenue.

Years ago, when my children were too small to pay attention, I'd often found excuses to drive by that old garage apartment and reminisce, but it had been ages since I'd been in that neighborhood. As the memories came back to me, it was suddenly inconceivable that Naomi and I had let so much time go by without contact. What had happened to us?

"You've certainly done quite well for yourself," I offered after an awkward silence. "Your last book was my favorite."

"You've kept up with me, too." I heard the smile in Naomi's voice before she plunged ahead. "All day I've been asking myself how we could have let so many years go by. Beth, are you going to go back?"

Truthfully, even thinking about Kay's letter made my palms sweat. A stubborn part of me wanted to argue that I never thought of our mother, much less cared about whatever she'd made of her life after we were gone. But another part of me, the part that sat in the lamplight gripping a lukewarm bottle of wine night after night, knew better.

"I don't know," I answered Naomi, but I did know. I didn't want to go. "It's been so long," I said. "I'm not sure I want to reopen any old wounds." *Or create any*, I thought. *I don't want to create wounds for anyone else.* "Maybe it's best to leave it alone." Then, because it was expected, I returned the question, "What do you think?"

"I think we should go," Naomi answered, saying exactly what I had feared. "From what Kay says, this might be our last chance to put the past to rest. You know, I can hardly even remember what it was like growing up there. I was so young when we left, not quite sixteen years old. Isn't that crazy? I don't even know what it is we're supposed to be putting to rest."

"Naomi ..." I began, but she cut me off.

"Sometimes I'm afraid it was a mistake," she said. "Leaving, I mean. I left my entire life behind and I don't even know why. I know it wasn't the best childhood; I haven't forgotten everything, but was it really so bad we had to leave?"

Silence stretched across the miles as she waited, but I didn't know how to answer her. In Cedar Hollow and no doubt well beyond, Pritchetts had spent generations building a reputation that was impossible to shed. Mention the name *Pritchett* to nearly anyone in those parts and they'll inevitably have a story to share, not just about whiskey running and illegal activities, but about drunken brawls and countless other outlandish behaviors.

I grew up surrounded by these things, but I grew up surrounded by good things, too. There's something to be said for having a strong sense of family, even if the family is a crazy one. *It takes a village*, they say, and I'd definitely had that. I'd never known any other place like it.

Was it really so bad we had to leave? I couldn't answer that for Naomi. What I knew was at the time I chose to leave it seemed the only choice I could make.

The silence stretched on until, apparently giving up on an answer from me, Naomi asked a different question. "Beth, do you ever think of Luke?"

I'd thought about little else the past forty-eight hours. I think Naomi chose to follow me onto that train because she hadn't wanted to be left alone to deal with the dysfunction that was our family, but me, I left because of Luke. Or more accurately, because of his death. I squeezed my eyes shut tight against the memory, as if I could magically block it out. God knows, after twenty-seven years you'd think I'd have learned that wouldn't work.

I suppose I had thought—or hoped, at least—if I could just put enough distance between me and Cedar Hollow, I could erase the memory of Luke's death. I couldn't, of course. If anything, the older I got the more vivid the memories became.

The last night of Luke's life had colored everything I'd done from that point on. The thought of returning to Cedar

Hollow made me dizzy; the memory of Luke made me physically ill. I dropped to my haunches on the tiled kitchen floor, resting my face against the cool stainless steel of the refrigerator. I felt an involuntary wave of anger towards Naomi for invading my safety zone. Cedar Hollow had no place in my ultramodern kitchen, nestled within my admittedly ostentatious house, settled safely within my upscale southern neighborhood.

"Beth? Are you there?"

I switched the phone to my other hand. "I'm here, Naomi. I just ... I'm not sure I can do it." Through the receiver pressed to my ear I heard Naomi exhale. She was disappointed; I remembered that sigh.

"Come on, Beth, I don't want to go alone. Let's do this together."

"Naomi," I said, vaguely saddened that after so many years of absence it took a mere ten minutes of reconnection for me to become irritated, and her to become disappointed. "I'm just not sure going back is a good idea. Besides, Marissa needs me here. Mark is always at work, and she's going through a little bit of a rebellious period. I don't think it would be good for me to leave her alone just now." All of that was true, and I hoped Naomi would accept those excuses without further argument. It didn't take long for me to realize I'd forgotten how stubborn my baby sister could be.

"Bring her along," she said.

"What? Naomi, I can't just ..."

"Sure you can. Think about it. It'll be a bonding experience." Naomi warmed to her argument. "You can reconnect with your daughter at the same time you introduce her to relatives she's never met, very interesting relatives, I might add. Just imagine what her 'What I Did for Summer Vacation' essay will be like. It sounds to me like a perfect opportunity."

Behind me, I heard movement on the stairs and quickly stood. Lightheaded, I leaned against the refrigerator for support, hoping my pose looked casual rather than desperate. Marissa had apparently chosen that moment to finally get up and ready for her appointment. "Let me think about it," I said to Naomi. "I'll also need to discuss it with Mark. Will you be around tonight?"

I heard Naomi rustling through what sounded like a mound of papers. "I have a conference call with my publisher this evening, but I should be done by eight at the latest. I think that's seven your time. Will that work?"

I had no idea whether or not Mark would be home by then, but I agreed anyway. I needed to get Marissa to her appointment, and I certainly didn't want to have this discussion with Marissa poking around in the kitchen looking for her breakfast. "I'll call you then," I told Naomi.

I hung up the phone and turned to Marissa, surprised to see her dressed already. "Who was that?" she asked, as she rummaged through the refrigerator with one hand in search of milk, a bowl of cereal precariously balanced in the other.

"Your Aunt Naomi." As much as my answer amazed Marissa, I think it amazed me even more. Marissa carefully set the milk on the counter and turned to look at me, her brown eyes wide. As always, I couldn't help but appreciate how beautiful my daughter was, petite and curvy, just coming into her own. The Pritchetts were many things, but physically unattractive wasn't one of them.

"Your sister?" She set the bowl of cereal on the counter alongside the milk, and pushed her long, dark hair out of her face.

"That's the one."

"You *called* her?" Her voice was disbelieving.

"Actually, she called me." I felt an adolescent stab of pleasure with that simple remark. Naomi had called *me*.

"But ... *why*?" The lack of sensitivity demonstrated by teenagers cannot be overstated. Several responses sprang to mind: *Because I'm her sister? Because she missed me? Because, in spite of everything, she thinks I'm a person worth calling?* But I said none of those.

What I said instead was, "We'll talk about it on the way. Hurry up and eat your cereal, and for heaven's sake, don't forget to brush your teeth. Remember last time they said you weren't brushing well enough around the brackets. Get a move on; we're running late."

Marissa rolled her eyes and leisurely spooned a mouthful of cereal from the overflowing bowl, milk dribbling down her chin. Funny I'd never noticed, until recently, how much she resembled her Aunt Naomi.

Chapter 5

Geraldine Porter Pritchett

I hear them whispering, and I know what they're saying. *Crazy*, they say. *Lost her mind.* Folks always did accuse me of being weak. I know well enough what they said behind my back all them years, while they was smiling at my face. I know what they say now. This little town ain't big enough to hide things. But I ain't weak and there ain't nothing wrong with my mind, and goddamn them all to hell and back for saying there is.

Tell me this: When a person is done living, what's crazy about dying? I lost my Junior a year ago last month, and I lost my children too many years ago to count. I have outlived and outlasted anyone or anything I ever cared about, and I am finished; there ain't nothing weak about that. There ain't nothing crazy about it, either, but I'll be damned if just when I decided I was done with it all, Kay Langley didn't go and call my girls home. And what right had she to do that?

She told me what she'd done when she stopped by to bring me some supper from the diner. I was glad to see Kay; there was a time we was close, and the beef stew she brought tempted my appetite for the first time in weeks. I even managed to swallow a little of it down, to please her, if nothing else. Kay comes from a long line of good cooks and good people, but it wasn't good of her to meddle between me and my girls.

If I'd known she was doing it, I'd have told her not to. The last time I heard anything at all about my girls was through Kay, just over a year ago when their daddy died. She called them home then, too, but they didn't come, and I don't imagine they will now. I reckon it's clear they didn't care for their daddy; I reckon it's also clear they don't care for me. Maybe he didn't deserve their caring. Maybe I don't, either. Maybe I don't, after all.

My girls left me without a word just after Luke's funeral. I remember hearing later how we broke the heat record that day, but I didn't notice it at the time. I didn't feel the heat, and I didn't care about no record breaking. I stood there in that terrible sun in the cemetery behind Cedar Hollow Baptist Church, and watched them put my boy in the ground, and I felt anger, boiling hotter than any heat wave, rising up in my chest like the steam from one of them goddamned stills.

I was mad at God and at Junior and at every Pritchett that ever walked the earth, but most of all I was mad at myself. I was so full of boiling over anger I couldn't hardly speak, much less shake the hands and hug the shoulders of those who came to pay their respects. *Repects*, I remember thinking at the time. *Not a goddamned one of you respects us, so there ain't no use in pretending now.* But I swallowed my pride and took their offered hands, because that wasn't the day to make my stand. I didn't leave Luke's grave until every last crumb of dirt was put over him and all the hypocrites was gone. Then I climbed up into that rattletrap truck of Junior's and let him take me home.

When we got there I walked right past all them people, all the good ladies of the church with their covered dishes and the men in their Sunday shirts with sweat stains spreading under their armpits and around their collars. Lord knew, they hadn't ever attempted to set foot in my house before my boy's funeral, and I didn't see the need for them to be there, then. I didn't say a word to nobody, and truthfully, if I'd given in to the angry impulses in my mind, I'd have shot them all dead where they stood. But I didn't. Instead, I shut my door and stripped out of my clothes and climbed into bed, even though it wasn't but two o'clock in the afternoon and the sun was shining into that bedroom hot enough to peel the paper on the walls. I laid there and stared at the water-stained ceiling above the bed until the room grew too dark to see.

Every now and then I heard car engines start, and the voices grew less and less until finally the only ones I heard were those of Junior and his brothers, and after a while even those went away, far enough from my window that I could pretend they was gone for good. When Junior opened the door to come to bed I moved for the first time all evening.

"Get the hell out of here," I said, turning my head away from him. "And close the door back behind you."

Junior Pritchett hadn't listened to a word I'd said in the twenty years of our marriage, but he listened to me that night. He pulled his head back and shut the door and left me be. I stayed right there just like that until the next afternoon when I remembered I had a husband and two other children who needed me; remembering that forced me from my bed, though in truth I didn't want to go. But I couldn't be done with it all just yet, no matter how angry I was.

That was when I learned the girls wasn't nowhere to be found. Junior didn't know where they was, and not a single member of his whole goddamned worthless family had even noticed them going. "Now calm down, Geraldine," he told me when I raised my voice, accusing every last one of them of being the white trash they was known to be. He reached out for me, but I swatted his hand away.

"I don't want to calm down," I told him, "I want my girls." I had just lost one baby; I wanted to keep the other ones close to me where I could see them. Maybe I knew what they'd done, even then, because my chest was already cinched up with fear.

Junior gave up on trying to calm me down and went to the diner to ask if anyone had seen my girls. Valerie Poindexter said she'd seen them headed toward the station when she opened up the library that morning. Kay Langley called over to the stationmaster who told her the girls had bought tickets to Memphis.

The stationmaster said they told him they was going to visit relatives to let them know in person about Luke's death. He said he figured we'd sent them so he didn't think nothing of it. But they'd lied; we hadn't sent them girls nowhere and didn't neither one of us have kin in Memphis.

A body can go through a lot of bad feelings in twenty-seven years and I reckon I've been through just about all of them. When something goes wrong in a family people look to the parents first, especially the momma, and it is true that a parent can kill the soul of a child. What people don't realize is that a child can also kill the soul of a parent. Yes, she can. I reckon I ought to know.

Kay had no business meddling between me and my girls.

Chapter 6

Naomi Pritchett Wells

My morning phone call with Beth left me churning in a sea of conflicting emotions. Clearly, she didn't want to return to Cedar Hollow; her voice sounded panicked even discussing the possibility. But I had spoken the truth when I'd told her I couldn't remember exactly why we'd left in the first place.

It wasn't easy growing up a Pritchett, and like any teen-aged girl I was full of adolescent angst, maybe more than most, given my family history. I was embarrassed by our circumstances, by the uneasy silence that fell among the men in the general store when my father walked in, by the pitying glances the women of Cedar Hollow cast in my mother's direction on the rare occasions she went to town.

Beth and I were children of the seventies, although aside from the colorful outfits worn by Valerie Poindexter, the town's young librarian, the seventies more or less skipped over Cedar Hollow. Monetarily speaking, nearly everyone I knew was poor. West Virginia had the distinction of being the only state covered in its entirety by President Kennedy's Appalachian Regional Commission; that's how poor we were.

If anyone in town had any money to speak of, it would have been the Haydens and the Poindexters. The town of Cedar Hollow was lucky in some ways. At a time when many small towns had limited access to medical care, we had rarely been without a doctor. Dr. Benjamin Leary had delivered both of my parents, and after he passed, Dr. Graham Hayden was lured from Huntington to Cedar Hollow as a result of the Appalachian Redevelopment Act of 1965. I'm sure Dr. Hayden has passed on by now, too, but on the rare occasions my siblings or I needed medical attention, it was to Dr. Hayden's office we went.

It wasn't until I was older and long gone from Cedar Hollow that I realized we must have been a charity case. I imagine many people were. We certainly didn't have health insurance or money—moonshining doesn't come with typical benefits—and Dr. Hayden never struck me as a man with a taste for 'shine. Even if he had been his wife, Sue Ann, would never have allowed it in her home.

I never knew her first husband, the one everyone said was quite a catch; he died in the war before their marriage really even got started. Her second husband, however, was very well known by my family. Jimmy Williamson had been a raging alcoholic with a penchant for violence, one of our biggest customers until he disappeared in '75, leaving Sue Ann and her son, J.J., to fend for themselves until Dr. Hayden convinced her to try marriage for the third time. No, moonshine was not an option for Dr. Hayden, and since moonshine was all we had to give, I can only assume Dr. Hayden went unpaid.

During my final years in Cedar Hollow, we were also fortunate enough to have a dentist, something nearly unheard of at that time outside of the major cities of West Virginia. Valerie Poindexter—Burnett at that time—came to work at the Cedar Hollow Library in 1975 to earn credits for her degree at Marshall University. I later learned that it was the good women of Cedar Hollow Baptist Church who petitioned Marshall and recruited Valerie for their "Bring Literacy to Cedar Hollow" campaign. At any rate, to everyone's surprise Valerie fell in love with our little town, and managed to talk her fiancé, Dr. Thomas Poindexter, into joining her upon his discharge from the service at the conclusion of the war in Vietnam.

We Pritchetts knew Valerie, of course, but we never had occasion to step into Dr. Poindexter's office. In the Pritchett household, toothaches were taken care of exactly as one would expect, with a stereotypical shot of whiskey and, on more than one particularly memorable occasion, a set of pliers. Having witnessed our unlucky cousins' screams, Beth, Luke and I decided not to mention any oral troubles we might be experiencing.

As children, Beth and I had gazed in awe upon the brick houses of the Haydens and the Poindexters. Three or four times a year Valerie Poindexter invited the children from town to her home for a story hour, and Beth and I attended well past the age I'm sure Valerie had intended. We sat in a circle with the other children on the brown shag carpet of her living room, working our toes through the thick pile, munching on homemade chocolate chip cookies and drinking grape Kool-Aid while we listened to Valerie read from books that were much too young for us.

On the long walks home, we promised each other that someday we'd have a house as fine as the Poindexter home, with wall-to-wall carpeting and furniture that matched, furniture that wasn't worn down to the wood on the ends of the arms, the stuffing spilling out of the frayed upholstery. Built-in glass holders, my father used to say, setting his glass on the exposed wooden frame of the arm, the sweat leaving permanent circular stains on the wood. Aren't we mighty fine, now! How odd that I just remembered that about my father.

We were poor, but not really much poorer than the majority of the people in Cedar Hollow. What set the Pritchetts apart wasn't the lack of money. It was harder than that to define. There's a dignity that often goes along with poverty, a stubborn sense of pride inherent to the American psyche, a refusal to accept charity and an insistence on pulling oneself up by one's bootstraps.

That's what was missing in the Pritchetts; that's what set us apart from our neighbors. We embraced our chaos and filth and reveled in our reputation as hard-drinking, law-breaking rebels. Upon reflection, I supposed at some point throughout the generations Pritchetts must have realized deviance was all they had, and subsequently decided to embrace it as a point of pride. Our neighbors were impoverished and dignified; we were trash, and proud of it. That was the difference.

I was an emotional child, very different from the hardened cousins, aunts and uncles that always seemed to surround me. I cried over hooked worms and hyperventilated when the men skinned and gutted the live fish they caught in Rugged Creek. I ran screaming when chickens were caught, refusing to watch as their heads were chopped off in preparation for dinner. And I fought and shouted and begged, my stomach in knots, when the babies of the family were introduced to taster duty.

I was an oddity, and for that I was teased and tormented. It was a difficult childhood made even more difficult by my differences. Yet, my question to Beth remained unanswered even in my own heart: Had it really been so bad we had to leave? Kay's letter had forced me to reconsider my past, and for the first time, I was tortured by doubts. In spite of the difficulties I had faced as a child, I had never felt unloved. Not even once.

The phone rang in the dark silence of my office. Evan had gone to bed hours earlier; it was nearly midnight. Beth's number popped up on the screen, and I clicked the on button before it could ring a second time.

"Hello?"

"Okay," she said. "I'll go. I'll call tomorrow and we'll make plans."

And that was all. She'd disconnected, leaving me alone in my dark office to wonder at the frayed edges of her words, that slight slurring that was such a part of my childhood.

Chapter 7

Beth Pritchett Sloan

"Hurry up, Marissa!" I was aggravated, sweating through my linen jacket in the smothering Memphis humidity. It was barely nine o'clock in the morning, and already hotter than Hades. The extra glass of wine the previous night wasn't helping matters. As I struggled to load my overweight suitcase into the back of the car I felt vaguely nauseous, greasy in spite of my morning shower.

Our flight was at eleven. Allowing time to park, check in, and hike to the terminal, we barely had enough time to make it. Marissa, however, remained maddeningly unconcerned.

"Chill, Mom. It's all good," she said, as she sauntered out the front door in a warring cloud of fragrances, dangerously low midriff bared to the world. I bit my tongue against the angry responses knocking at my front teeth, and pretended not to see the tattoo on her pelvic bone, just noticeable over the low slung waist of her cut-off shorts. I had expressly forbidden any tattoos, but I had enough to worry about at that moment without instigating a new battle with Marissa.

I could still hardly believe Marissa was coming with me to West Virginia. When Naomi had first suggested it, I'd had two warring thoughts: first, that I didn't want to go myself, much less drag my daughter along, and second, that Marissa would never want to leave her friends and home during summer vacation to travel a week with her mother—the horror—to a tiny little mountain hamlet the likes of which she'd never seen.

About my second assumption I couldn't have been more wrong. As soon as I'd broached the subject with Marissa she'd jumped at the opportunity. I must admit, I was touched that her curiosity regarding my childhood and family of origin seemed genuine, but also concerned that she might be assigning a bit too much romanticism to the entire affair. I couldn't fault her for that; it was the typical response I received from people on the rare occasions I spoke of my upbringing.

Truthfully, there really *was* a sort of romanticism about the way I was raised. Rogue hillbillies, illegal activities, secrets … all made for a good story, if not for a great childhood. Even the setting was ideal, not just the rickety shack and the hidden stills, but the imposing mountains and lush flora. I'd grown up close enough to Rugged Creek to dangle my feet in it from our front porch during the spring rains, and more than once we'd slept on the roof to escape the waters when they overflowed their banks, a makeshift tarp stretched over our heads.

On such nights, Naomi and I had lain on our backs, watching the clouds scuttling across the sky through the holes in our dry-rotted tarp, making a game of identifying any constellations lucky enough to make an appearance. We always imagined we could touch those constellations, hitching a ride on Taurus the Bull or taking flight with Aquila the Eagle, if only we could just stretch a little further. Even then, Naomi had a talent for words, a penchant for drama, although I don't think we'd recognized its complexity. She spun fanciful stories about bedazzled chariots and flying horses as I lay quietly, lost in the seductive web woven by her voice.

Luke, too, made up stories, but his were of a mischievous sort. He relished scaring us with tales of Sasquatch or escaped madmen, all of whom he swore were hiding in the shadows just behind the closest tree. Every time the branches rustled in the wind we shivered with delicious fear, clinging to each other as if this could somehow protect us, warding off the evil Luke invited with his tales.

During calmer moments, we basked in the cool nighttime breezes, swatting mosquitos away from our ears while we listened to the frogs, temporarily dislocated from their normal haunts beside the creek, chirruping in the front yard. One year the water rose so high we could hear it lapping against the front of the house from our pallet on the roof. We spent hours pretending to be on a yacht somewhere in the middle of the ocean, tossed about by the waves. The next morning we found a dead trout just inside the front door.

We looked forward to our spring nights on the roof for all those reasons, but also because that was one of the few times we didn't have relatives camped all over the yard. I didn't know where they went, but there wasn't room for them on the roof and the added weight on the rusted tin would have surely caved it in. When the creek overflowed they disappeared as if swallowed up by the dark woods, and at least for a day or two, we had our home to ourselves.

These were the kinds of stories that held Marissa spellbound as a little girl, and it was these stories she no doubt envisioned when she thought forward to our trip. To a girl who grew up in the suburbs outside of a major metropolitan area, mountain trails, cold creek water and shady relatives made for high drama, and more than once I heard her excited whispers on the phone as she discussed our trip with her friends.

In Marissa's eyes, Naomi and I had grown up the female equivalents of Huckleberry Finn, and now she was about to experience some of that herself. It was flattering to have her sudden interest and attention. Over the past year or so, our main modes of communication had been either screaming matches or stilted silences. To have her not only engaged in real conversation, but actively pursuing it, was immensely gratifying. I was able to see past the challenge of her teenage years, back to the sweet little girl she'd always been. Even more satisfying, I caught glimpses of the lovely young woman she would soon become.

Her enthusiasm also amused me; the closest Marissa had ever come to any sort of a rugged existence was at church camp, where she bunked in an air-conditioned cabin with five other girls and a camp counselor. Marissa imagined herself wading through Rugged Creek and hiking mountain trails, but I knew my daughter would never stand for the cool mud squishing between her toes or the gnats swarming her eyes. I let her chatter on, however, without interjecting my thoughts. I didn't want to test the fragile bond her curiosity had forged, and she'd find out her limitations soon enough on her own.

In the midst of Marissa's excitement, I struggled to ensure she fully understood the real reason for our trip. She knew, of course, that I'd been estranged from my family since before she was born. She knew I'd lost a younger brother, and that my father had passed away the previous year. She was thrilled at the prospect of finally meeting her Aunt Naomi, and although she was aware the reason for this reunion was my mother's reported mental decline, I wasn't sure she really understood the gravity of the situation.

That concerned me. I didn't know what to expect from my mother, and I wasn't sure I wanted Marissa to be witness to whatever I was about to encounter. Mark and I had had several discussions regarding the matter, until we'd finally decided to allow Marissa to accompany me. In all likelihood, this would be the only chance she ever had to meet my mother, and whatever my mother's faults had been, violence had never been one of them. Instead, passivity was her sin. Had my father been alive, our decision would have been different. Then again, had my father been alive, I would not have been going at all.

I wasn't worried about Marissa's physical safety around my mother; I was, however, worried about her emotional safety. After all, I was taking her into a world my younger sister and I had chosen to leave, not only because of the punishments doled out by my father, but also because of what we—or I, at least—had always seen as supreme indifference on the part of my mother.

"The difference," Mark had pointed out, "is that she has you."

As distant as Mark and I had grown over the past few years, I was oddly touched by his vote of confidence. He was right; Marissa had me, and I vowed to remove her from any situation I deemed to be too stressful or upsetting for her. In the end, Mark and I agreed that the positives of allowing Marissa to meet my family outweighed the negatives.

Marissa was aware of our discussion and concerns, sometimes actively participating, other times simply listening. I sensed that in some way she enjoyed watching her father and me discuss the issues, perhaps because it had been such a long time since we'd shared any meaningful conversation. What Marissa didn't know, but desperately wanted to know, was what had happened to drive my family apart in the first place. I wasn't sure I would ever be able to answer those questions, partly because I didn't know all the answers myself.

"Mom?"

I startled, drawn from my thoughts, and turned to see Marissa close beside me, a look of concern etched across her face. "Mom, are you okay?" She set her bags on the ground.

"Of course." I tugged at my too-tight jacket, smoothing out the wrinkles. I had recently acquired a couple of extra pounds that stubbornly refused to leave, but I rejected the impulse to buy new clothes. Doing so would have seemed like surrender. "Is this everything?" I shoved her suitcases on top of my own. She nodded.

"Mom ..."

I turned to look more closely at her. She was chewing the inside of her cheek the way she often did when something worried her, and I wondered if she was finally beginning to understand the seriousness of our trip. "What? Are you having second thoughts about going?"

Marissa stared at me a moment longer, frowning, and then shook her head. "No, it's not that. It's just ..."

"Yes?"

"Nothing. Never mind, it's all good."

I hesitated, briefly tempted to press her for more, but ultimately deciding against it. Her awkwardness indicated whatever it was she had on her mind probably wouldn't be a pleasant thing for me to hear, so with a guilty sense of relief I let it go. I'm often a coward when it comes to seeing myself through Marissa's eyes.

"Okay then," I said, slamming the trunk. "Get in, and let's get this show on the road." I was eager to get through the chaos of check-in and boarding. I hoped to grab a quick nap on the plane, hoped even more that if I did, the bags under my eyes would disappear. I was nervous about meeting Naomi, and even more nervous about what she would think of me.

Glancing at my watch I saw that, barring any unforeseen circumstances, we had plenty of time to make our flight. Naomi had scheduled her flight to arrive in Huntington at nearly the same time as ours. From there, we'd take a rental car to Cedar Hollow, where we'd arranged to stay at Erma Puckett's boarding home, Vines and Roses, in rooms close to our mother's. After that, I had no idea. I was afraid to even speculate.

Chapter 8

Kay Langley

A bright reflection through the front window caught my attention as I was wiping down tables, and I looked up to see a white van pulling into the handicapped spot by the door. Seeing that van gave my heart a lift, I tell you; it was the children from up on the mountain, the ones at Jessie McIntosh's Platte Lodge for Children. I hurried back to put up my dishrag and wash off my hands. "Riva," I yelled over to the diner's only waitress, "it's the kids comin' by for a milkshake."

Riva poked her head around from the kitchen to see. "Well, I'll be." She pulled off the plastic gloves she'd been wearing to cut up vegetables and grabbed a fresh pair out of the box on the shelf. Me and Riva had known each other since we was girls. At one time we'd thought my Andrew and her girl Sandra might marry, but we'd been wrong about that, and it was probably for the best. I don't know as our friendship could have survived being in-laws. I love Riva, but we can both be a might stubborn when it comes to our kids.

Now she came walking around the counter to join me. "I was wonderin' when they was goin' to show up this time. You think Robby's with them?"

I checked the clock on the wall over the door. "I expect he is. Isabelle don't get off work at Dr. Poindexter's until five, and you know Jessie ain't goin' to allow nobody else to take care of Robby."

Robby was Robby O'Brien, grandson of June and Raymond O'Brien. Raymond and June had practically raised Robby from the time he was born until they both passed away this past year just after Robby turned ten. Isabelle, Robby's momma, had a rough period for a while, but she was starting to come together all right.

The lodge Jessie had built up on Billy May's mountain was for children with disabilities, and Robby had Down syndrome, so Jessie was somehow able to finagle it so Robby could stay at the lodge while his momma worked. That's where Jessie got to know Robby, was up at the lodge, and she did love that little boy. Jessie couldn't have no kids of her own, you know, so she just took Robby right up under her wing.

Riva and I stood watching out the window as Virgil Young, the van driver, lowered the chairlift and assisted a little girl out of the back. It was good to see Virgil back at work, and even better to see how much happier he looked now that his wife was on the mend. They'd gone through a mighty hard time, Virgil and Mary, but things seemed to be headed in the right direction for them now. Mary was feeling better, putting on a little bit of weight and getting some color back in her cheeks.

"There he is!" Riva pointed, and sure enough there was my little Robby, jumping down the step to the parking lot, turning back to wait for a friend. "And there's Jessie, too. I didn't know she was in town this week."

"She just got in yesterday," I told Riva. "To see the kids before they leave."

"She bring that man of hers with her?" Riva squinted out the window and leaned to the side as if she could somehow see into the van better that way.

"Not this time," I told her. "Jessie said he's got so many projects goin' on he can't hardly keep up, especially since she's cut back on her workload and been recommendin' Michael to take her place." We moved behind the counter and began getting ready to make the shakes.

Robby was the first one through the door with his big old smile, his red hair damp with sweat from the hot summer day. I swear I don't know what it is about that child, but he does warm my heart. "How's my boy?" I asked him as he scooted up onto a stool, his knobby little white knees poking out from under his shorts.

"Good, Mrs. Kay. Can I have chocolate please?"

"You sure can. How's your momma doin'?" I had to raise my voice over the bustle of children being seated. I was pleased to see his face light up at the mention of his momma.

"She's great," he answered, twisting side to side on the stool. I leaned close to make out what he was saying. Robby has a hard time getting his words out right, and sometimes he talks soft because of it. "She's coming here to pick me up when she gets off work," he said, and I understood him just fine.

"She'll be here in about twenty minutes, just in time for you to finish your shake." That was Jessie, helping another little boy with thick glasses and a hearing aid get settled on the stool beside Robby. The lodge serves a different group of kids every week, except for Robby, and I enjoy getting to meet all of them when they stop in for a treat.

Jessie was looking good, healthy and tan with her hair pulled back in a ponytail. Seems to me the older Jessie gets, the happier she gets, and it's about time. Watching her help the counselors get the kids settled with spoons and straws, I could see she was finally starting to put her past to rest for good. When the children was all seen to, Jessie turned to me, leaning forward across the counter.

"Kay, I could have sworn I just saw Beth and Naomi Pritchett getting gas at Mr. Smith's." Mr. Smith's General Store, she meant, though it hadn't been Mr. Smith's for a long, long time. Jessie actually owns the store now, but it's run by Dennis Lane, along with his daddy Darryl. Darryl is officially retired, but retirement don't seem to mean much these days.

"Is that possible?" Jessie was asking. "I know it's been a long time; it might not be them."

So they'd made it. I hadn't heard back from either one of them, but I had heard a rumor that they'd been in touch with Erma Puckett about some rooms at the boarding home. I nodded at Jessie. "It's them," I said. "Come back to see their momma."

For a minute, Jessie didn't say nothing, just stood there looking perplexed. I knew how she felt; it was hard to know what to say. It was just one of them situations where everybody is sort of right and everybody is sort of wrong all at the same time. I wouldn't say Geraldine and Junior was careful with their kids, exactly, but I wouldn't say they set out to mistreat them, either.

Geraldine and Junior grew up during hard times, there ain't no doubt about that, and things was different back then, not just in Cedar Hollow but everywhere. Why, I didn't know hardly anybody my age—our age—who hadn't been whupped with a belt at some point as a child, unless their parents had a preference for a switch instead. "Kay, go get me a switch," my momma would say when I'd sassed her one too many times, and I'd go do as she said. I had a good momma; I knew she loved me; that's just the way it was.

What I'm meaning to say is the way children was raised back in my day was different from what it is today. We was expected to work, and there was always something needed doing, whether it was chopping the garden, digging post holes, or hanging wash. That's how we lived; didn't nobody think much of it.

By the time most of us was grown with kids of our own we realized there was different ways to raise a child from the way we'd been raised. But the Pritchetts stayed to themselves so much, they just kept on doing things the way things had always been done to them. Geraldine might not have grown up as hard as Junior had, but you put even the hardiest flower in the middle of Mile-a-minute weed and it'll get choked out every time, especially if that flower has been so sheltered it don't know what to do out in all that fresh air.

Geraldine, bless her heart, wasn't the hardiest flower to start with. She was not a good student in school; Geraldine was known more for being pretty than she was for being clever. But that ain't all of it. She was a follower, Geraldine was. I reckon she didn't know how to do anything *but* follow, with her momma and daddy controlling her the way they did. They kept a tight hold on Geraldine—too tight, if the truth be known.

We was friends back then, much as we could be. We sat under the elm together at lunch, and we played hopscotch and jumped rope together at recess. Geraldine always took care not to get dirty or mussed; her momma didn't allow for an untidy look. Every now and then we was known to pass a note or two back and forth during class, particularly if we had our eye on some boy or another. I enjoyed what little time I saw Geraldine, but I didn't see her at all outside of school; none of us did. Her momma and daddy kept her close to home.

The best I can figure, they must have been in their forties before Geraldine come along; they was quite a bit older than my own parents had been. Rumor had it Mrs. Porter had lost several babies before coming to term, and that would surely explain why they was so protective of Geraldine. We could see her sometimes, when we was all outside together, the group of us, you know. She was just about always sitting at her desk by the window, reading or sewing, or sometimes just looking out at us. We'd motion for her to come along, but she never did. She'd shake her head, pointing back over her shoulder, letting us know her momma and daddy didn't want her running wild, taking a chance on getting hurt.

She was such a meek girl, I don't know how she ever got up the courage to go off with Junior, though knowing how Junior was, he probably didn't give her much choice. Leastways, that's what we told ourselves at the time; it was the only way we could understand it. Once she took up with him, she just switched from following the directions of her parents to following the directions of Junior. No doubt his directions was the worst of the two, but Geraldine couldn't see that at the time, though the rest of us saw it plain as day.

Given what they'd come from, I don't think Geraldine and Junior intended to mistreat their kids; that's just the only way they knew to do. They worked their children hard and, on some occasions, Junior was known to keep them in line with a belt. They wasn't inclined to shower love on their babies; Junior'd been raised to believe loving on a child meant spoiling it, and Geraldine … well, I don't imagine Geraldine had the best idea of what love should look like, either. In some ways, I think that was worse for them kids than any whuppings they may have got. They kind of all just took care of themselves.

Many was the time they showed up in town and it was clear they hadn't bathed in a while. Andrew told me about one time when Luke got in a fight at school because a boy made fun of the way he smelled. Bless his heart, Luke was a good-looking boy; he just hadn't been taught.

I know that sort of thing made life hard for the girls. Beth worked for me in the diner for a short time before they run away, and I know she didn't have no one telling her how to fix her hair or put on lipstick the way young girls like to do. I wanted to help her, but I didn't know exactly how to do it without hurting her feelings. And then she was gone.

But here's what I mean about everybody being right and everybody being wrong. Beth and Naomi was right to want to leave their situation; like I said before, couldn't nobody blame them for that. But they was wrong to leave their momma the way they did, and right after Luke died, too.

Geraldine lost all three of her children at the same time and she grieved hard, I know she did. She hadn't always been the way she was after she got surrounded by Pritchetts; there was a time she knew better, but that was when she was sur-rounded by her own family. I think to Geraldine's way of thinking, she was trying to let the girls have the room they needed to grow. By the time the stationmaster tracked the girls down and let Geraldine and Junior know where they was at, she had decided—or, more likely, Junior had decided for her—if the girls was happier gone, they'd leave them be until the girls decided on their own they wanted to return home. I don't reckon she realized, way back then, that time would nev-er come.

I understood Jessie standing there not knowing what to say about it all, because I didn't know what to say about it all, either. I just hoped it hadn't been a mistake, me calling them girls back like I did.

Chapter 9

Naomi Pritchett Wells

I had been stunned by Beth's appearance, but I struggled not to show it. My flight had been the first to land at Huntington Tri-State Airport and, as we had agreed, I collected my bag, arranged for the rental car, and then settled in to wait for her at The Landing Restaurant, picking at a salad and using the time to check email and touch base with Evan.

Evan had offered to travel with me, but I refused. I had no idea what was in store for me—for any of us—but I felt more comfortable facing it alone. Evan had heard stories about my childhood, stories often enhanced for comic or dramatic effect, but his quiet, studious existence was so far removed from the reality of the manner in which I'd been raised that I couldn't imagine subjecting him to it. As I sat in the restaurant, too nervous to eat, I was engulfed by a deep sadness, a profound sense of loss and regret.

I still remembered everything about the morning Beth and I left home. I awakened in the gray dawn to Beth shaking my shoulder, hissing at me to hurry up and dress. Already—or maybe it was still—it was hot enough that the sheets were damp with sweat, the humidity causing my hair to curl in damp ringlets about my face. Although we slept with the window open, there was no breeze to provide relief; not even the treetops were moving against the dark sky.

Until Luke's death we had not planned to leave, or at least I hadn't; I don't know about Beth. The plan had taken shape the night of the funeral as we lay on our bed, sweating in our panties and t-shirts, silent with our thoughts. I had found it impossible to reconcile Luke's absence with his death. It wasn't unusual for Luke to be gone overnight during the summer months. Camping, fishing, hunting—the men and boys in our family, Luke included, often left for a night or two at a time, returning with sometimes a fresh kill, sometimes nothing at all other than the reek of whiskey oozing out of the men's pores. I kept expecting Luke to return any moment, teasing me to come and watch him skin his latest catch, knowing full well I'd scream and run the other way.

Luke was a tease, but not a mean-spirited one. In spite of the fact that he was younger than we were, as the only boy he considered it his duty to shield us from any harm that ventured our way, whether that was something as benign as a wayward rat snake slithering through the henhouse, or as feared as a turn with our father's belt. More than once Luke had saved me from Daddy's anger when my inability to do as I was told meant certain trouble.

One incident that stands out above all others occurred shortly before we lost Luke, when it was my turn to guard the mash barrel. There was never a shortage of wildlife around our place, and the large amounts of corn and cane sugar guaranteed a constant rat population, particularly during fermentation when spillings covered the ground. Daddy's brother, my Uncle Wayne, once swore he saw a rat drunk on teedum, and it wouldn't surprise me if it were true. I do know it wasn't unusual during bad infestations to see tooth marks all along the barrel, sometimes deep enough to puncture the wood.

At any rate, one of the tasks my siblings and I were assigned was that of keeping rats away during the three-day period it took for fermentation to be completed. We had traps, of course, but the ratio of traps to rats was woefully inadequate; therefore, it was up to my siblings and me to guard the barrels. Specifically, we were to club to death any rats careless enough to venture into the open. Of all the jobs we were charged with, I despised that one the most. I was terrified of the rats, even more so of the snakes that inevitably came along with them, but I was absolutely incapable of killing them in spite of knowing that refusal to do as my father ordered meant facing his wrath.

It was one day that final summer that Luke found me sitting high atop the stepladder, as far away from the ground as I could get, holding the club and crying. "Go on," he'd said with a sigh of resignation and a jerk of his head. "I got it."

And I'd gone gratefully, searching for some way to pay him in return, maybe by hoeing his share of corn, or maybe by grinding it, a terrible job guaranteed to lead to blisters and sore muscles, but to me, preferable to clubbing rats to death. At least the corn didn't know it was being beaten and took its punishment in silence. Although he often teased me about my tender heart, Luke alone, of all my family members, seemed to understand; that was enough to make any blisters or sore muscles I suffered well worth the effort.

The moonshine making business ground to a temporary halt the day of Luke's funeral, the mash forgotten in the barrels, the rats given free reign. My mother had gone silently to her room and closed the door as soon as we'd arrived home, and I remember I'd envied her that solitude.

The afternoon stretched interminably, until finally the last relatives had wandered out to the yard, leaving us in peace. We watched our father open the door to their bedroom and then close it softly without entering. He hesitated for a moment, glanced at us briefly, and then let himself quietly out the back door, joining the pack of voices murmuring in the dark beyond the kitchen window.

Beth and I had cleared away the empty plates and crumpled napkins, emptying ashtrays and wiping down counters. "Should we take her some food?" Beth had asked, nodding towards the closed bedroom door.

I shook my head. "I think she wants to be left alone." I would not have disturbed my mother; she was not the type of woman to be disturbed. If she wanted something, she let us know. Her silence spoke as loudly as her words.

Later, in the dark of our bedroom, Beth had propped herself up on her elbow, looking down at me, her face beaded with sweat in the heavy night air. "Naomi," she said, "let's leave."

At first I thought she meant leave the stifling heat of the house, taking a blanket and going in search of a breeze by the creek. We often did that on nights we found it too hot to sleep. "I'm too tired, Beth," I had answered her. "Besides, it's just as hot out there, and we'd never be able to sneak past them all." I scooted farther away from her, from the heat radiating from her body, searching in vain for a draft of air.

She shook her head in the moonlight, and I could see damp strands of hair sticking to her cheeks. "I mean really leave. I've got some money saved away from the diner. Let's leave, Naomi."

I don't remember stopping to think about the consequences of what Beth was suggesting. I was emotionally exhausted, still traumatized by the loss of my brother. I was old enough to understand the circumstances of my life and feel trapped by them. I chafed at the stigma of my surname, was embarrassed to be part of a family that seemed determined to live up to every negative stereotype conjured up by the state motto we'd learned in school, *Montani Semper Liberi*. Mountaineers are always free, my uncles loved to say, but I doubted Mr. Diss Debar's idea of freedom and my uncles' ideas had much in common, particularly since my uncles' definitions tended to fall on the wrong side of the law. I longed to be anywhere but where I was at that moment, and so when Beth proposed that we leave the next morning, I agreed.

I didn't think ahead; I had no plan. If someone had told me I wouldn't see my mother again for decades I wouldn't have believed them; the thought would have been incomprehensible. I suppose I thought, if I thought at all, that Beth and I would escape the suffocating sadness, the unbearable silence of my mother, the incessant presence of my relatives for a day or two until I could breathe again. I just wanted a breath of air, I remember thinking. Just a breath of air.

And so, that next morning, I got up when Beth told me to. We dressed quickly and noiselessly, throwing the remainder of our clothes into a battered suitcase that had once belonged to our grandmother. Beth eased open our bedroom door and peeked out, wincing at the creak of the hinge. The house was quiet, stale cigarette smoke from the night before still drifting under the yellowed ceiling. I touched Beth on the shoulder and pointed towards the window, but Beth shook her head. We had no way of knowing who might be camped out under our window; we had less chance of getting caught by going out the front door. We tiptoed into the silent hallway, alert for any evidence of our mother. Her door remained closed.

I don't remember my thoughts as we hurried down the worn dirt path beside the creek, following it to the gravel road at the foot of the mountain. What I do remember is that my chest felt lighter. I glanced over at Beth to see if she felt the same, but her expression was closed to me, her face a blank mask. I struggled to keep up with her, the cardboard suitcase banging against my knees. At the station I barely registered the lies Beth told, in a hurry to get on the train, the destination unimportant to me, the fear of getting caught overwhelming.

We were silent on the trip, no giddy laughter at having successfully escaped, no excited plans for what we'd do once we arrived in Memphis. In hindsight, I don't think I believed we'd ever really make it to Memphis. Someone would come after us, and our brief streak of rebellion would end. We'd be home by nightfall, no doubt with strap marks across our backsides. But they didn't come after us. They never did.

My cell phone vibrated against the table and I jumped, snatching it up, catapulted back to the present, remembering that Beth and I were now traveling in reverse. It was her; she and Marissa had arrived. I stood, peering toward the entrance of the restaurant, ready to wave them over to my table.

I saw them before they saw me. If I hadn't been expecting Beth, if instead I had simply passed by the tired looking woman in the wrinkled linen suit on some busy sidewalk, I would not have known it was Beth. This middle-aged woman with the puffy face, the skin bruised and thin around swollen eyes, was unknown to me. But there was no mistaking Marissa, even though I'd never seen so much as a photo of her.

With a jolt, I realized Marissa was almost exactly the age Beth had been when we left Cedar Hollow. It was like stepping back in time, the resemblance to her mother—the young version of her mother—was so strong. I struggled to regain my mental balance as Beth turned toward me. Her gaze landed on me and I wondered if she, too, would be taken aback by changes wrought by the passage of time. If she was, she covered it well. I took a deep breath as they made their way to the table.

For better or worse, there we were.

Chapter 10

Geraldine Porter Pritchett

I hear them out there, my girls. Betsy, my Home Health nurse, has bathed me and washed my hair and now she helps me into my gown, the soft flannel one that keeps me warm. Junior bought me that gown the last winter he was with me. It's worn nearly through now, the section in front of my knees without its yellow color, the daisies faded away, nearly see-through in its thinness. But I wear it anyway.

I know what people thought about Junior; I know what they think about all the Pritchetts. Hell, haven't I thought the same things myself too many times to count? But I loved him; I did. He was a hard man, but just when I knew I couldn't possibly take no more, when I knew I must surely break, he'd do something like buy me a soft flannel gown with a daisy print to keep me warm at night. Junior had a tender side, but not many people aside from me ever saw it.

I always knew about the Pritchetts, of course, but I didn't know Junior until I got old enough for my momma and daddy to decide I could finally walk downtown by myself. I was near about seventeen years old, by then. Junior was older than I was, and he hung out with a rough crowd, leastways as much as we had rough crowds, or crowds at all, in Cedar Hollow.

I was a late in life baby for my momma and daddy. The Porters all seemed to have a hard time with having babies, and by the time I come along my momma and daddy had given up on having any kids of their own. They was surprised to learn about me at that late stage, but they'd always wanted children, and there I was.

I reckon because I'd been so hard to come by, they protected me like I was made out of fine China. There ain't no doubt I was a pampered child, but pampered and spoiled ain't the same thing. I knew even as a young'un that Momma's role was more about her own ideas than it was about me. She always trimmed my dresses with ruffles and lace and plaited my hair with ribbons, and it frustrated her to no end that no matter how hard she worked at it, I never could stay clean and pressed for more than a minute or two.

But her attentions had nothing to do with the child I was. I hated them dresses, the starched lace so rough against my skin. I longed to tear them from my body, freeing my hair from the braids that pulled so hard against my scalp. No matter how much I begged, Momma wouldn't allow it. That wasn't the idea she had in her head about what being a good momma was all about. To her way of thinking, a good momma had good-looking children, clean and combed and dressed up nice.

She wanted me to do quiet things, safe things, like reading and sewing, but I wanted to go outside like the other children. I used to watch them riding by on their bicycles, dirty bare feet pumping the pedals, fishing poles tied to the handlebars, and wish more than anything I could go with them instead of being where I was, holed up at the study desk in our dark living room, reading, or hunched over needlepoint or embroidery or some other useless activity Momma thought I should learn. It kept me safe, there ain't no doubt about that. But for what?

I hadn't never ridden a bike or set foot in Rugged Creek, but I'd heard stories of kids riding out to the creek on hot West Virginia days, daring each other to jump off the bridge into that cold, clear water, swimming out there along with the turtles and fish. I wanted, more than anything, to feel that breathless feeling I heard those kids talk about when they jumped into the creek while the water was high, before the spring temperature was right.

I was jealous of them kids, it's true, of the easy way they spoke to each other. They'd come to school on Monday mornings fresh-faced from their time in the clean mountain air, plumb full of stories about frog gigging and fishing, of sleepovers and birthday parties. I sat and listened, pale-faced and shy in my pinafore and saddle oxfords. They wasn't mean to me; I just wasn't a part of them because I wasn't allowed to be.

I know Momma loved me and wanted to protect me in her own way, I know she did, but there was times during my childhood when I felt plumb suffocated by that kind of love. I imagine that's why Junior Pritchett was so attractive to me. He was wild; he was everything my momma had tried to keep me from, all rolled up into one big strapping man.

The first time I noticed him, once I was old enough to notice men in that way, he was slouched against the wall outside of Peggy's Diner with his hair slicked back and a cigarette hanging from his mouth. He looked right at me and smiled, a slow, wicked smile, and I felt a pull that never did let me go.

I broke their hearts, falling in with the Pritchetts, but what I felt for Junior was just too strong for me to resist. He was freedom to me; I imagined the way I felt when he smiled at me was something akin to what them kids always talked about, that breathless shock of Rugged Creek the first time they jumped in of a season. Junior was all those things my Momma had denied me, which was exactly why I loved him. I miss him even now.

Betsy kneels down to pull socks over my feet to keep off the chill. Erma Puckett says it's right hot outside these days, but Betsy knows I'm always cold. Betsy has a way of knowing what I need without me even saying, which is good because I am no longer moved to speak. While Betsy works on me she don't notice the footsteps in the hallway, don't pay no attention to the whispers passing by my door.

But I do, and I know it's my girls. Lord, I heard those same noises often enough that summer before they left me, when they'd sneak out at night to go down to the creek for some air. They always thought I didn't pay no attention, but I did. Of course I did.

Some nights it was all I could do not to join them, leaving Junior's sweating, snoring self alone in our bed and heading for the cool night air with my children. In my mind's eye I could picture them laying back on a blanket under the stars, swatting at mosquitos and whispering, maybe about boys, or maybe about me. They'd laugh low, shushing each other so as not to be found out. Luke, too, used to sneak out at night, sometimes alone and sometimes with Naomi trailing along behind. Oh, yes, I knew. I always knew.

I don't know what it was made my children long so for the nighttime. Maybe it was because the air seemed so much lighter at night, when all them Pritchetts was finally quiet. Or maybe it was because they could move easy without worrying about me and Junior forever fussing at them and giving them chores to do. Whatever it was, some part deep inside me understood it, and maybe even felt it, too. Nights like that, listening to them tiptoe out the door, my bedroom felt like a prison to me, just like my childhood had. But I didn't follow; I stayed behind.

If I had given in to my urge to join them, if I had walked barefoot through the wet grass and appeared at the side of their blanket, it would have ended. They would have clammed right up, jumping to their feet to face me, afraid of me and my punishments. Their eyes would have gone big and wide and they'd have tripped over their words, desperate to explain to me what they was doing out of bed and down by the creek at such an unholy hour. The magic spell would have been broken. That's why I left them be.

I didn't want to be their momma on them nights. I didn't want to be the one to make them hush up and go to bed. What I wanted was to plop right down beside them. I wanted to feel the breeze against my face, up underneath my gown, whispering with them and laughing about whatever it was they laughed about. I wanted to run through the moonlight the way I'd seen Luke and Naomi do when they thought they was hidden from me. I wonder if things might have turned out different had I asked them to show me the stars they was always looking at, or to tell me one of them stories they whispered about to each other up on the roof. I might have asked them what they laughed about when they thought no one could hear.

But I didn't do them things, much as I might have wanted to. I didn't want to suffocate them the way my momma had suffocated me. I wanted them to have the freedom to enjoy the night air without me forever breathing over them, the freedom to dip their feet in the water without me warning them about snakes and leeches and God only knows what other things was surely waiting to get ahold of them. I didn't want to bury them in my questions, making them feel like they couldn't have a single thought all to themselves.

I didn't join them in their foolishness, but I didn't let it come to nobody else's attention, either. I kept their secret. It was the best I knew to do. Junior never found out, and I shudder even now to think what he might have done if he'd known about their nighttime shenanigans.

I always knew what folks around town said about me, what some still say. Said I let my kids run wild and didn't take proper care of them. Said I didn't love them the way I should have. But that was a lie. I did love my children; I loved them so much I didn't want to squash the life out of them like had been done to me. I loved them so much I kept secrets from my husband, who would have surely strapped the joy right out of them if he'd known.

On those endless nights I stayed in the house in that go-dawful heat, laying next to Junior and waiting on the night to end so I could get up and start another day, which would be just like the last one had been and just like the next one would be. Like all the days had been, right up until the day after Luke's birthday, when they pulled his dead and broken body from out of the creek.

That's right; it was his birthday the night my Luke died. We never had money for fancy presents, but I always managed to get them all a little something on their birthdays. For Luke, it was a Swiss Army knife, one with all the gadgets. He'd had his eye on one behind the glass counter at the general store for weeks.

Billy May Platte was running the store by then; Mr. Smith had passed on. She held onto one of them knives for me special and kept it until I went to collect it that morning. She wrapped it up for Luke in the Sunday comics, and that touched me, that she'd done that for him. After I went and got it, I set it on the table next to Luke's cake, a Mississippi mud cake just like he'd asked for. I'd gotten up at sunrise to make that cake for Luke.

Every one of us had a piece of it after dinner, singing "Happy Birthday" to him while he blew out all thirteen candles. The day of Luke's funeral a part of that cake was still sitting on my kitchen counter, surrounded by the casseroles and cakes brought by the women of the church. There wasn't much of it left, but it sat there leaning over on the plate, dark and melted and looking to me just like the muddy bank of Rugged Creek where they'd drug my boy out.

I don't know who finally threw that cake away, but I ain't never baked another one since. And wasn't it something, I thought back then, that the whole of my life I'd wanted nothing more than to splash in Rugged Creek, first with the children I'd known as a girl, and then with the children I'd borne from my own womb. And at the end of it all, that goddamned creek had taken my boy. Wasn't it something, I said to myself. Wasn't it something, after all.

Betsy finishes with my hair and props me up in the chair by the window, settling me with an afghan over my knees. The sun is setting out over the mountains and it's getting late. Betsy will let me sit here and watch it for a little while, and then she'll help me to my bed.

I have grown old in this town, along with all the children I used to envy. They got married, too, just like I did, and had their own babies. I watched their children grow up and start families, and I tried not to think of everything I was missing with my own girls, maybe married themselves and giving me grandbabies I'd never know.

Junior kept me going, sometimes by fussing at me and sometimes by holding onto me. Junior's way of grieving was different than mine. He hurt deep over losing Luke, but as for the girls, he just plumb erased them from his memory, never said their names again and wouldn't allow me to, either. Junior was like that; he didn't take betrayal kindly, and that's what he felt like the girls had done to him. I wonder what he would think about them showing up now. I doubt he'd stand for it, to tell you the truth.

Erma asked me if she could bring my girls to see me this evening, and I shook my head no. We can do whatever it is we need to do tomorrow. They need time to get settled in, and I don't have the strength for it tonight. They'll also need time to work up the courage to see me, just like I need to work up my courage to see them. I don't know what scares me more, the idea that I might feel too much when I see my girls, or the idea that I might not feel anything at all.

Chapter 11

Beth Pritchett Sloan

I closed the door behind me, the swollen wood sticking slightly in the frame, finally giving way and latching with a soft *screech*. The sound immediately brought back memories of the wooden doors in the house in which my siblings and I grew up. The bathroom door had been the worst, swollen not only from the outside humidity but also from the steam from the nearly boiling hot showers Luke suddenly began taking that last year of his life.

Nearly every Sunday morning, after what seemed an eternity, Luke would finally emerge, his skin flushed red from the hot sting of the spray, grinning at whichever one of us stood glaring at him, our knees clamped together, bladder straining for release. More than once Naomi and I had been forced to run for the woods, crouching behind a bush for relief while Luke steamed his way through all the hot water in the tank.

I leaned back against the door of my rented room at the boarding home and dropped my suitcase on the floor in front of me, exhausted. The flight itself was uneventful. We'd encountered no problems with our electronic tickets, our luggage or security. We'd settled into our seats in plenty of time, relieved to see a scattering of empty rows. Once we were in the air, I had planned to stake a claim to one of those empty rows and stretch out for a nap, still desperate to rid myself of the tired circles under my eyes.

I had just reached for my purse to turn off my cell phone for the flight when the phone rang. Glancing down, I saw Mark's familiar number across the screen, and I hesitated. I had considered sending the call straight into voicemail; Mark would simply assume we were already in flight. It wasn't that I didn't want to speak with Mark; it was more that I didn't have anything to say. We'd discussed Marissa and agreed she could come with me. What else was there?

Sometime over the last year, or maybe even longer—yes, definitely longer—our conversations had become stilted and awkward, as if we realized that now the children were nearly grown, we had very little to say to one another. It was distinctly odd, particularly given the animated discussions and debates we'd had before the children were born. Back then, we'd taken smug satisfaction in the caliber of our dialogues, in the endless supply of entertaining and thought-provoking subjects about which to converse.

We'd sit up late into the night, wine in hand, and set forth our theories about the origin of the universe, the state of the economy, the similarities between Hinduism and Buddhism. We'd linger over our empty plates at the little café down the street, the one where we'd met, our coffee gone cold, neither of us willing to break the spell cast by our words, oblivious to the irritation of the wait staff eager to turn the table over to another potential tipper.

"Look at that poor couple," we'd say, shaking our heads and clicking our tongues, cutting our eyes towards a middle-aged couple alone in their silence by the front window. "So sad they have nothing to say to each other," we'd murmur, comfortable in the superiority of our youth. "That will never be us."

And then the children came along, and our conversations turned from philosophy to formula, from politics to play dates. It didn't happen all at once; it happened with a series of first times: the first time Mark was too tired to stay up and share a glass of wine with me, the first time I was too tired to awaken early and linger over coffee with him, the first time everyone was too busy to sit and share dinner together. In the beginning it saddened me, as I imagine it did Mark. But gradually the sadness turned into gratitude for that extra twenty minutes of sleep, or reading, or just plain solitude.

Without even trying, we became that silent middle-aged couple by the front window of the café. "How pretentious they sound," we now say of the younger couple, cozy at the back table, engrossed in discussion. We shake our heads and roll our eyes. "Young people think they know everything." And then we smile at each other and return to our silence, comforting ourselves with the counterfeit superiority borne of age, too weary from it all to reach for each other across the chasm.

"Is it Dad?" Marissa had shifted in her seat to look down at the screen of my phone. I nodded and clicked to accept the call.

"Did you make it in time?" The deep bass of Mark's voice had filled my ear, the words soft with concern, and I updated him on the negligible quest of our check-in and boarding experience. Satisfied that we were safely on our way, Mark had said what we've always said before ending phone calls, "I love you. You guys be safe."

"You, too," I had answered, as I always did, and then I sensed a slight hesitation from Mark. "What?" I asked. "Did you need something else?"

"No," Mark had said. And then again, "No. Call if you need anything. I'll miss you."

I had handed the phone off to Marissa and been amazed, as always, by the way her voice changed when she spoke with her father. Whereas I considered myself lucky to get more than a grunt from Marissa most days, she was all excited chatter with her father.

I had turned to the window, eager to leave Memphis but not eager to arrive in Huntington. I had wished, as I gazed out the window at the baggage handlers loading the plane, we could fly forever in a state of suspended animation, somewhere high above the earth, detached from all the things that shackled me to it. I didn't see how I could survive a return to Cedar Hollow; Luke's ghost would be everywhere.

But the plane had indeed landed, and there I was, in Vines and Roses Boarding Home, just next door to Marissa and across the hall from Naomi. Our mother, Erma Puckett had informed us, was down the hall to the left, in the room across from the bathroom. "But she's busy right now," she said, placing a warm, brown hand on my arm. "Home Health is here. Why don't you ladies get settled in and make yourselves comfortable. Will you be eating with us tonight?"

I hadn't given a thought to where we'd take our meals, and I glanced at Naomi just in time to catch her smile. "Beth, let's go to Peggy's Diner," she said. "Wouldn't it be nice to see Kay?"

Before I could answer Marissa jumped in. "The place with the key lime pie! Oh, Mom, we have to go there. Aunt Naomi, Mom has been talking about Peggy's Diner my whole life."

Already my sister and my daughter were forging a bond, with me on the opposing side. Without my input, the matter of where to eat was settled, except that I seemed to be having trouble moving. I needed to unpack and was dying to get out of that bothersome linen suit, but I couldn't seem to pull myself away from the door. From my vantage point I took in the room: polished hardwood floor, scattered braid rugs, quilted spread on the queen-sized bed, fresh flowers on the nightstand. Cozy, comfortable, and utterly terrifying.

Once, when Matthew was thirteen, he was injured during a game of middle school football. From my spot on the bleachers I saw him go down, and I knew immediately it was bad. Mark wasn't there; it was one of the few games he ever missed, but he'd been called away by an emergency early that morning. At the collective gasp of the crowd I turned to a friend, another mother whose son was also playing, and barely registered the look of horror on her face as I said, "Take care of Marissa."

She nodded, her hand to her mouth. "Oh, Beth," she said, and then I was gone, flying down the mountain of bleachers, sprinting along the side of the field to the gate, pushing my way past players and coaches and out onto the field with Matthew. I shoved someone—I don't know who it was—aside and knelt down beside my son.

His turned towards me, panting, his eyes huge and dark in his pale face, sweat droplets beading on his forehead. He reached for me. "Mom," he said. "My leg." He thrashed on the ground as hands reached out to keep him still, gently removing his helmet and pinning him down to keep him from moving. "It hurts." He arched his back, his voice shrill, spiraling out of control, his teeth clenched against the pain.

I grasped his hand, squeezing it in my own. "I know, Matt. I know. Don't look." I put my free hand against his cheek and forced him to face me, my eyes only inches from his. "Look at me. Look only at me."

And he did, my brave boy. He kept his eyes locked on my face as the paramedics worked over him, as he was loaded into the ambulance, as we rushed, sirens screaming, towards the hospital where Mark would meet us. And the whole time, his dark eyes were questioning me. *Can't you make it stop? Aren't you going to help me? Why aren't you fixing this?*

It was the same look Luke had given me the last time I saw him alive. It was what had kept me away from Cedar Hollow all those years. How could I face my mother, after the look Luke had given me?

Chapter 12

Kay Langley

"Well, would you look at that."

I turned from the counter where I'd been refilling salt shakers to see what Riva was talking about. Beth Pritchett was practically dancing down the sidewalk towards the diner, pointing up at the mountains, skipping ahead of the two women behind her. But then I came to my senses and realized that couldn't be Beth; Beth would be in her forties by now. And Beth wouldn't have never worn them tiny little shorts this girl was wearing. Lord have mercy, the child was barely covered. And was that an earring in her bellybutton reflecting the sun back at me?

"She's the spittin' image, ain't she? Except for the way she's dressed, I mean." I set down the salt canister and went to stand beside Riva.

Riva grunted agreement. "Except she looks happy. I don't recall Beth ever lookin' happy, do you?"

I don't reckon I did. So if this was the daughter of one of the girls, that meant the two women behind her was the girls. As they got closer, I could see that Naomi looked as much the same as a person can after so much time. She was still trim like she'd always been, and she still had that open look about her, like she was just waiting to see what might happen next and thinking it might be good. Her hair was still dark, but cut short like a pixie. It looked right cute on her, I thought.

Beth, though, she had changed. She was two years older than Naomi but she looked a whole lot older than that. She had put on some weight, but not too much. Her hair was cut short, too, but it was more gray than black. Could be that Naomi colored hers and Beth didn't; that wasn't really what made Beth look old. No, it was her face that had changed so much.

I could still see the girl in there, but I had to look past the puffy eyes to do it. She had deep frown lines over her nose and around her mouth; she did not look like a happy woman, that's for sure. What she looked like—and I hope the good Lord'll forgive me for saying this—was the worst of the Pritchetts. Old Man Pritchett, to be exact. Lucas senior. Hard and unhappy and ... well, I'll just say it: like Old Man Pritchett always looked after he'd been hitting the 'shine a little too hard. It made me sad, seeing Beth that way.

"They're comin' this way, Riva." I picked up the tray of shakers to get them put back on the tables before the girls made it to the door. It was just after suppertime and the diner was nearly empty, Jessie and the children long gone. Andrew was in the back cleaning off the grill, and my daughter-in-law, Teresa, was helping their daughter Hannah roll napkins at a table in the rear. It was quiet right then, but as soon as word got out that the Pritchett girls was back in town and sitting in my diner I knew half the town would suddenly have a craving for a cup of coffee and a piece of pie. Funny how that works.

I got back up to the counter just as they come in, the little bell tinkling up above their heads. Naomi took one look at me and practically jumped into my arms, bless her heart. She always was a bighearted girl. When she let me go, Beth stepped in and gave me a little squeeze, but she stepped back real quick, like she didn't want to get too close to me. Beth never was as outgoing as Naomi, but the woman standing in front of me looked downright brittle, like she might break in half any minute.

Before I could think what to say to her, the young one stepped right in front of her momma and put her arms around me, too. "I'm Marissa," she told me, "and I've heard about this diner my whole life. I'm so excited to be here." She pulled back to look at me and she was grinning ear to ear. If her momma was looking like the worst of the Pritchetts, she was looking like the best, that girl was. She was a pretty thing, with her dark hair curling all around her head and her eyes shining at me. She looked like Beth used to look, but she was Naomi all over, and that was the difference.

"And I am glad to finally meet you," I told her, smiling back. "Just what has your momma told you about my diner?"

"That you have the best key lime pie in West Virginia, and that you were good to her and my Aunt Naomi." She twisted her hands together in front of her bare belly, all of a sudden shy with me. I don't know how a girl can show that much skin and still be shy, but she was.

"Well, you'll have to try my pie tonight, then, and let me know what you think. Have you all eaten yet? No? Riva, let's get these ladies seated and get them somethin' to eat."

Just as Riva moved to seat them, the bell tinkled above the door again, twice in a row. Just as I had thought, it was about to get real busy in my diner. For the next hour Riva and me was running our feet off. It got so busy at one point we had to ask Teresa to step in and help us, her eight months pregnant and all.

While Riva and me was running orders I kept an eye on Beth and Naomi's table. Most of the townsfolk stopped by to chat with them; Darryl Lane and Eugene Cooper, Valerie and Dr. Poindexter, Corinne Johnson—people was just glad to see them after so many years and pleased they'd finally come home to see their momma. Wayne and Wally sat with them for a long time, catching up on things, and Virgil and Mary Young joined them for a little while, too. Virgil and their daddy, Junior, had been friends when they was younger, though Virgil hadn't never been quite as wild as Junior.

Naomi chatted with everybody, standing up to hug people, leaning over to hold hands. The girl, Marissa, was even more excited to meet people than Naomi was. She was sure enough happy to meet her kin, I can tell you that; she was smiling so big it near about split her face in half.

Beth, though, she just sat quiet for the most part, and I felt my heart going out to her. Something was bothering her; that much I knew. As I pondered over it she looked up, straight at me, catching me off guard, and the look on her face was so troubled it near about broke my heart.

I couldn't help myself; I set my tray down and walked over to the table, pushing my way through the crowd, and pulled Beth up by her hands, wrapping my arms around her tight. She stiffened up at first, but then she relaxed and hugged me back, laying her head against my shoulder. I felt her sigh. "I never wanted to come back here," she said. Underneath it all she was still the unhappy little girl who'd left us all them years ago.

I held onto her and patted her back. "Have you seen your momma yet?" I asked.

She shook her head against my neck and I felt her blow out a long breath. "No. I don't think I can do it, Kay."

I held her away from me to look at her face; her hands was cold and sweaty in my own. Around us the people was still talking and laughing, paying no attention to us. Beth refused to meet my eyes. "What in the world is it, Beth?" She didn't answer, just kept looking down at the floor and shaking her head.

"I don't know what's goin' on, Beth, but I will tell you this: Your momma is a broken woman. If there's any peace you can give her, you need to do it. Whatever she did—whatever they did—to you, you have to let it go. Do you understand what I'm sayin' to you?"

That got her attention, and she looked at me for a second. "It isn't just what they did to me, Kay. It's also what I did to them."

She let go of my hands and sat back down, crossing her arms over her chest and turning away from me to watch Marissa, who was deep in conversation with Valerie Poindexter. I stood there for a minute thinking on what she'd said. I wanted to help her, but I didn't have no idea what to do.

I went back to taking orders and cleaning tables until the diner finally cleared out and the last dish was put away. Andrew took his tired family home while Riva and I closed up for the night.

"You ready to get out of here?" Riva retrieved her purse from the cubby under the counter and tossed her soiled apron in with the laundry.

I shook my head. "Not yet, but you go on home."

She squinted at me before smiling. "I reckon you've got some thinkin' to do. Don't think too long. Tomorrow's likely to be a busy day." She gave a little wave as she let herself out the door.

Riva was right; I had some thinking to do. There was something peaceful about my diner late at night when everything was quiet. It was comforting to me, the hum of the refrigerators, the soft glow of the security light. It wasn't lonely because it was almost like all the spirits of them people was still there, talking and laughing and communing with each other. But at the same time, I could be alone with my thoughts without little hands pulling at me for this or that, or Howard asking me where was his fishing hat, or could I pack him a lunch for the next day.

It was in the dark in my diner that I'd sat and worried over Andrew when he'd flunked out of history his junior year in high school. It was there I'd cried when I'd first learned Emily was pregnant at the age of eighteen with no boyfriend in sight. It was also there I'd worked at the books, making sure we could make it on one income when Howard was ready to leave the rails.

Even though there wasn't no longer anyone at home to pull on me and distract me from my thinking, it was still where I liked to be when something was weighing on my mind, and Beth was surely weighing heavy on my mind that night.

Chapter 13

Naomi Pritchett Wells

By some unspoken agreement, maybe simply following the ingrained pattern of tagging along after my older sister, the three of us ended up back in Beth's room at the boarding home, kicking off our shoes and flopping onto the queen-sized bed as if, instead of two middle-aged women with a teenaged girl in tow, Beth and I were ourselves again teenagers, snuggling in for a night of gossip and pillow fights.

In truth, and in spite of the warring emotions overwhelming me since receiving Kay's letter, I was happy to be sharing that moment with them. I found Marissa delightful, vivacious and full of curiosity, and after my initial surprise at Beth's appearance, I'd come to recognize her younger self in her mannerisms and expressions. Even the fretful way she held herself struck a familiar chord. I'd forgotten how fragile Beth had sometimes seemed to be. I'd experienced many frustrated moments with her when we were children, pushing and prodding her to move past her anxiety and participate in whatever fun Luke and I had managed to scrounge up between chores and family responsibilities.

Perhaps her timidity was one reason I'd not taken the initial hours of our escape from Cedar Hollow seriously. I was the spontaneous one, the one known to make impulsive decisions based on emotion. Beth was the worrier, always borrowing trouble, our mother used to say. Packing up and sneaking out at the break of dawn was completely out of character for her. Some part of me, even now, found it hard to believe we'd stepped aboard that train, effectively ending not only our family, but our childhood as well.

After leaving the diner, Beth, Marissa and I had walked through the tiny town, enjoying the evening breeze and the view of the mountains, sharing memories with Marissa. The library, the old school, Cedar Hollow Baptist Church, each seemed to conjure forth a story, and we took our time reaching Vines and Roses. Upon our return, Erma had intercepted us on our way to our rooms, letting us know, her voice quiet, our mother was sleeping. She agreed to send for us in the morning after the Home Health nurse was gone, when our mother was dressed and ready.

"Does she know we're here?" I had asked Erma, butterflies flitting around my stomach in a mixture of nervousness and anticipation. Suddenly, I wanted more than anything to see my mother. After all the years away, it was hard to believe she was resting just down the hall; I found it almost unbearable to have to wait another moment. The sense of loss I'd felt earlier was lodged in my chest like a stone.

As the steamy Memphis days had gone by and no one had come searching for us, my initial sense of relief at having escaped had turned to a disbelieving sadness. Although I had been the one to leave, I felt deeply hurt, abandoned by my parents. They didn't care for me, for surely if they had, they would have come. Kay Langley managed to track us down and keep up with us over the years; why couldn't our parents have done the same?

Eventually, the sadness hardened into a stubborn knot of anger. If they didn't care enough to come for me, I didn't care enough to return to them. All of this, of course, had been when I was much younger, before I learned that life is made up of subtle shades of gray, long before I relinquished the egocentric view of a discontented teenager.

I had thrown myself into my new life, shoving thoughts of home and family into the back recesses of my mind, scribbling poems and short stories late into the night in my little bedroom above the garage of the modest house in Midtown as an outlet for my pain. I made new friends, pursued my new passion for writing, and carved out a life for myself completely re-moved from the one I'd left behind in Cedar Hollow.

Somehow along the way even Beth and I had lost touch, the unraveled ties of our family too weak to hold us together. When I'd met Evan, I'd told myself I was finally complete with a family of my own. It had almost worked, this calculated ef-fort to remove my family from memory. Almost, but not quite.

Now that I was close to the age my mother had been when we left, surrounded by all I'd left behind, I found myself won-dering how she must have felt. What had she thought, the day after her only son's funeral, when she'd arisen to find she'd lost her daughters as well? The questions caused me to flinch with shame, the hard knot of anger I'd quietly carried for so long revealed for what it was: an all-encompassing grief, for Luke, for my parents and Beth, and for me. Looking back from the perspective of a grown woman, the losses were heartrend-ing, devastating in their pointlessness.

In front of me on the staircase Erma had nodded at my question. "She knows. She'll be waiting for you in the morn-ing." She reached out to squeeze my arm as we continued to our rooms, and I was grateful for the gesture.

Beside me on the bed, Marissa sighed with what sounded like contentment. Seeking out Beth over the top of Marissa's head, I raised my brows. This was the girl about whom Beth had expressed such worry? Catching my glance, Beth shrugged, raising her brows in turn, smiling at her daughter.

"How many cousins do I have?" Marissa was asking. "I counted at least nine tonight at the diner, but I know there must be more."

As Beth led Marissa through the crooked branches of our family tree, I couldn't help but wonder what both of them were really thinking. Not only had Beth experienced the same losses as I, she had also kept Marissa from a huge extended family, me included. Sitting up on the bed and facing her mother, Marissa struggled to pair the right children with the correct set of parents while I watched her from the side. If

Marissa felt any resentment, it didn't show. Her expression was curious, her forehead creased in concentration.

Across from me Beth laughed at the difficulty Marissa was having memorizing all the names, clearly enjoying the interaction with her daughter. To an onlooker, we would have no doubt appeared to be a normal family, mother and daughter and aunt, taking time out from our busy lives to maintain our close family bonds. But we were not as we appeared, and I wondered if Beth, or even Marissa, shared the suffocating regret I was feeling.

As Marissa chattered on, Beth suddenly sat up, snapping her fingers as if she'd just remembered something. "I nearly forgot," she said. "I brought something to celebrate our reunion." Standing from the bed, bending over and rummaging through her suitcase, she pulled out a bottle of wine, holding it triumphantly in the air.

Before I could respond, I sensed, rather than felt, Marissa tense beside me, and glanced in her direction. For the briefest of seconds, before she had a chance to close herself off and look away, I saw the truth, and I realized I wasn't the only one in turmoil.

Chapter 14

Marissa Elizabeth Sloan

My mother is a drunk. That's what I wanted to say to Aunt Naomi when Mom pulled out her stupid bottle. I didn't say it, though, because no matter how much she pisses me off, I do love my mom. It would feel sort of like betraying her to say something like that to Aunt Naomi. Besides, Aunt Naomi seems pretty cool, but I've only known her for like five hours; I don't know what she'd think, hearing that the older sister she hasn't seen in forever is an alcoholic. She might just think I'm a liar.

I first started thinking about Mom's drinking my freshman year at Germantown High, where I go to school. My best friend Stacey talked me into taking this class called Family and Consumer Science, where we talked about things like human development, family dynamics, that kind of stuff. One day Mrs. Davis, our teacher, asked us what we thought made a good family. I loved days like that, where we got to talk about things instead of just listening to a boring lecture and taking notes.

Anyway, we all basically said the same things, like good families listen to each other and respect each other, do things together, support each other, things like that. Stacey said she loved it that her parents always came to her dance recitals, and I guess that's what really got me thinking. Stacey and I have been taking dance forever; that's how we met. We weren't even in school yet when we took our first ballet class. I remember the first time I saw Stacey. How could I forget? She was the only one out of all of us that very first day who already knew how to do a perfect retire position. Most of us fell over trying, but Stacey stood perfectly balanced, right toes to left knee. Not even her dozens of hair ribbons moved.

Ballet was fun for a while; we loved to dress in sparkly outfits and have our moms curl our hair, but by the time we were in middle school what we were really into was jazz. By freshman year, Stacey was really, really good at it, and now that we're about to be seniors, she's already receiving scholarship offers. That's how good she is. I do okay, but not like Stacey.

She was right about her parents. They came to all of our recitals; they still do. Most of the time, they even stay during practice instead of dropping us off like a lot of parents do, and they actually watch us instead of talking on the phone or reading a book. Sometimes they even clap for us, and Stacey's dad is always yelling, "There you go, baby! You show 'em how it's done!" It embarrasses Stacey, but I think it's cool. They don't just cheer for Stacey; they cheer for both of us. You see how I keep saying *us*?

I sat in Mrs. Davis' class that day with Stacey trying to remember when my mom had stopped going to dance with me. I'd never really thought about it before. Riding to dance with Stacey had seemed normal, since we were always at each other's houses anyway. I could even remember Stacey riding with us a few times, too, but not in months. For some reason, I hadn't noticed until then that my mother never drove us anymore. I also hadn't noticed until then that Stacey hadn't been to my house in a long time.

I started counting. Out of the three recitals we'd had that year my dad had made it to two. It wasn't unusual for him to have to miss, depending on what was happening at his work. But my mom had only come to one. I thought back, trying to remember what she'd said. Headache, I thought. She'd missed the first one because of a headache.

I remember being a little bit worried about her when Stacey's parents dropped me off after that first recital because she'd been sitting alone in the dark. They'd let me out at the front walk and I'd noticed that Dad still wasn't home; his SUV was missing from the driveway where he always parked. Matthew was gone, too. He was almost always gone after he turned sixteen and got his driver's license. I was a little disappointed he wasn't home. I missed him. Matthew and I aren't like a lot of brothers and sisters. We get along really well; he's sort of like my best guy friend.

I let myself in, locking the door behind me and trying to be quiet in case Mom was sleeping. I didn't see her at first. I'd been crossing the living room to go up the stairs to my room when she scared me half to death, her voice coming out of the shadows over by the windows.

"How did it go?"

I'd jumped, dropping my equipment bag. "Good," I said, my heart just about pounding out of my chest. "It was good. You scared me." I peered through the gloom, trying to see her. I could barely make out her dark outline in front of the windows; the glow of the streetlights was behind her. At first I wondered why she was sitting in the dark, but then I thought maybe it had something to do with her headache. "How's your head?"

She didn't answer me right away. I heard a clinking sound, like a glass being set on the windowsill, something she would have fussed at me for doing. *Marble is porous*, she would have said to me. *Stop leaving your wet glass on it. Is it really so hard to take it to the dishwasher?*

"It's fine, Marissa," she finally answered. "My head is fine." She sounded weird, almost angry. Her voice left me feeling confused, like I'd done something wrong, but I knew I hadn't, not then.

"I'm glad," I told her, not knowing what else to say. She didn't say anything else, either, so I picked up my bag and continued up the stairs to my room. When I got up the next morning everything seemed back to normal, meaning Dad was at work, Matthew was still sleeping, and Mom was sitting by herself at the kitchen counter drinking coffee. When she saw me, she stood up to give me a hug.

"I'm sorry I didn't make your recital, honey. I don't know what happened, but my head was just killing me last night."

I squirmed out of her hug. Sometimes my mom can be too clingy, especially if she's apologizing for something. "It's fine," I said. "I'm glad you're feeling better." It really was fine. She'd never missed one before, and I knew she'd be at the next one.

The second time she missed my recital it was Stacey's mom who told me she wasn't coming. We were in Stacey's bedroom getting ready when Mrs. Yarbrough opened the door and stuck her head in. "Marissa, honey, your mom isn't feeling well." She held up a hand to stop me as I moved towards the door. "It's nothing serious," she said, "but she isn't going to make it to the recital. You can ride with us, and your dad will meet you there."

Somewhere in the back of my mind I remember feeling a little bit scared, wondering if maybe my mom had some deep, dark health secret she was keeping from us, like maybe cancer, or maybe muscular dystrophy, like my friend Jamie's mom found out she had a few years ago. Maybe she was trying to protect us by not telling us what was really wrong. After all, that was the second recital of mine she'd missed in just a few months because she was sick. But in the excitement of the recital and the fun of sleeping over with Stacey after it was over, I forgot all about it.

From the desk behind me in Family and Consumer Science class, Noah Gonzales made some crack about his family, something about step-siblings and bathrooms. Noah isn't nearly as funny as he thinks he is, so it was even easier than usual to tune him out that day. My classmates were still talking about perfect families, but I was realizing for the first time what was wrong with mine.

For the next few months it was all I could think about, like a light had come on and I was able to see things I hadn't seen before. I have friends whose parents never drink, but alcohol wasn't hidden in our house. Mom almost always drank wine with dinner, and most evenings Dad would have some sort of drink after dinner, something clear and sparkly in a little juice-type glass. We had a working bar down in the basement, and lots of times when Matthew and I were little our parents would have parties. Sometimes the parties were planned, but other times friends or neighbors just showed up out of the blue to visit. Matthew and I loved it when that happened because it meant we could stay up late playing with friends.

I had never thought anything of it when I saw my mom or my dad holding a drink. But after that day in class, I started noticing things, like how my dad would look at my mom, sitting by herself with a glass of wine, before shaking his head and telling Matthew and me goodnight, and how some mornings my mom didn't come down for breakfast before Matthew and I left for school. I noticed how tired my mom looked, and how she never laughed anymore. I realized we never had company, not even Matthew's friends, who used to drive me crazy, flopping all over the furniture in the family room, dropping food everywhere and taking over the T.V.

Once, I asked Matthew if he thought our mom had a drinking problem. "Well, duh," he said, stopping his video game to look at me. "She always has; it's just gotten worse lately."

I thought about that and realized he was right. My mom had always been the one to laugh the most and act the silliest during their parties. I hadn't known when I was little that that was a problem; I'd loved seeing my mom look so happy. She had also been the only mom who served wine to the other mothers instead of coffee or tea during play dates, something I wouldn't have even noticed except the moms all joked about how much they loved play dates at our house. My mom was the first one people called when they needed advice about what wine went with what meal, but I had been proud of her for that, because it seemed like such a classy thing to know.

The more I watched, the more I saw. I saw her sitting alone at night, staring out the front window and drinking her wine. I saw my dad watching her without saying anything, and I saw Matthew counting down the days until he finally left for college.

She never answered phone calls; she always ignored the doorbell. She stopped volunteering; she even stopped going to church. We never had company anymore and she never went out. It was like she didn't want to be bothered by anybody, not even us. It pissed me off that she wasn't there for me anymore, and it pissed me off even more when she jumped in with some kind of rule I was supposed to follow. Who was she to tell me how I should live?

Sitting in the Vines and Roses Boarding Home in Cedar Hollow, West Virginia, I didn't tell my Aunt Naomi anything; I just turned away so I wouldn't have to see my mother pop the cork. I had thought things might be different on the trip, but apparently I'd been wrong.

Chapter 15

Beth Pritchett Sloan

I'd barely stood with the bottle of wine before catching the look on Marissa's face. I must admit, it annoyed me. I love my children more than life itself, but there are times, more than a few of them, when I wonder if Mark and I made a mistake in the way we've raised them. The way Mark insisted we raise them.

I was twenty-one years old when Mark and I met, and I was immediately drawn to his thoughtfulness and sense of purpose. Perhaps it was because, at the age of thirty, he was older than I, or perhaps it was the heartbreak he witnessed during his residency at Le Bonheur Children's Hospital. For whatever reason, Mark was an old soul, wise beyond his age, a trait that I, as a rootless, directionless young woman, found irresistible. In turn, I think he enjoyed his role as protector of my vulnerability. I know he enjoyed teaching me, polishing up this hick from the hills. Mark's penchant for teaching me was what brought us together in the first place.

Naomi had moved on from waitressing by that time, though we hadn't yet completely lost touch. She had taken a job in a local bookstore, and on the rare occasions we connected, she talked incessantly about books. Naomi hadn't been a reader as a child, but then, she hadn't really had the opportunity. As a young woman, however, she immersed herself in books, her interest sparked, I believe, by the tattered copy of Jakes' *North and South* a customer had inadvertently left behind at the café in which we worked upon our arrival in Memphis.

By the time I met Mark, Naomi was studying for the General Educational Development test to get her high school diploma, something that was suddenly very important to her. She had also signed up for writing classes at the library. She seemed content to spend her off hours either reading or scribbling away in the notebook she always carried. I don't know what she scribbled, but I sometimes wondered if any of her musings from all those years ago had ended up in the stories she later published. At any rate, her sudden interest in books offered Naomi a direction for her life. Mark offered me a direction for mine.

The day I met Mark, I had just finished my shift and was posting a notice, advertising for a roommate, on the bulletin board in the front of the café. Finding bus schedules less than reliable, Naomi had moved closer to the bookstore, sharing an apartment with another bookstore employee, and my remaining roommates and I needed a fourth person to help with the rent. I pushed the thumbtack in place among the various notices regarding lost pets and furniture for sale, and turned to find myself face-to-chest with the quiet man I'd seen drinking coffee and flipping through papers at the back corner table.

"Don't you realize how dangerous that is?" His voice was deeper than I had anticipated, and he frowned down at me, dark brows drawn together over a nose just a tad too sharp. He pointed at the posted notice with a long, thin index finger.

I was flustered, and my face undoubtedly showed my confusion. *What* was dangerous? I needed a roommate, and advertising for one seemed logical. That's how things were done, where I'd grown up. If you needed something, you left a notice on the board at Mr. Smith's General Store. If someone had what you needed, they could either call or leave word at the counter, and you'd be notified on your next visit.

The stranger continued to look at me, his gaze uncomfortably direct. His hair was a tousled brown and in need of a cut, curling over the collar of a frayed blue button-down oxford shirt that was halfway tucked into the waistband of a beltless pair of khaki pants. He was pale, his limbs long and thin, and his eyes, behind gold wire-rimmed glasses, were a deep brown, the lashes long and curled. And he was still staring at me.

"You're not from here, are you?" That deep voice again, oddly incongruent with his appearance.

I shook my head. "West Virginia," I answered him. "Cedar Hollow, outside of Huntington."

"Ah," he said, as if that explained everything. "It isn't safe, advertising for a roommate this way. You never know what sort of person you could end up with."

It was on the tip of my tongue to tell him I doubted I'd attract anyone more colorful than the relatives with whom I'd spent my childhood, but I thought better of it at the last moment. There was something about this deep-voiced, slightly nerdy guy that I liked. I suppose that's why, when he gestured for me to re-enter the café with him, I did. He led me to his table and spent the next half-hour regaling me with tales about the dangers of big city life.

I hardly listened to what he said, caught up in the timbre of his voice and the earnest expression on his face. By the end of the conversation, I'd learned that his name was Mark Sloan and he was completing his residency at a local children's hospital. He knew a nursing assistant who might be a possible fit as a roommate; he'd give her my number. And, most importantly, he knew someone who knew someone who might be able to score a couple of tickets to the Orpheum Theater for a showing of *Cats.* Would I like to go?

I'd never heard of the Orpheum Theater and had no interest in a cat show. We'd had feral cats all around our shack, good mousers, my daddy used to call them, necessary to help keep the rodents out of the corn, but I'd always been slightly afraid of them. Nevertheless, I jumped at the chance to see Mark again, cats or no cats. Later, much later, my misunderstanding became a favorite inside joke, one of those affectionate stories to be shared at dinner parties to elicit gentle laughter.

Back then, I loved Mark's unshakable convictions. After having spent my childhood surrounded by utter pandemonium, Mark was an anchor in the storm, my knight in shining armor riding up to save me, not on a spirited white steed, but in an oil-belching green Ford Pinto. It was through Mark that I learned a different way of living, a structured way.

Through his eyes, I learned I could be a different person, a woman far removed from the tin-roofed shack on the banks of Rugged Creek. I was overjoyed to place my burdens on his shoulders, confident that he could take care of me, smoothing away the prickly trappings of my past and giving me a life such as Naomi and I had only dreamed about on our walks back from Valerie Poindexter's story hour. I had not known, back then, that his interest would sometimes feel an intrusion, that I would, at times, resent his scholarly approach to life, mine in particular.

In spite of his long hours, first to complete his residency, and then to strike out on his own, the first few years of our marriage were pure bliss. We were poor as church mice in the beginning. We lived in a dingy apartment in a seedy complex just outside of Midtown, and I decorated it with castoffs from garage sales and thrift stores, spending what little I earned from waitressing. In spite of the tackiness of the décor, it was beautiful to us.

Before we knew it, Mark's practice began to take off and I found out I was pregnant with Matthew. We were ecstatic, and Mark and I both agreed, back then, that I should devote myself to the children. After all, he reasoned, he could earn enough for all of us, and we needed to put the welfare of our children first.

Shortly before Matthew was born, I quit my job at the little café. A little over a year later, we bought our house in Germantown, and I became the epitome of a stay-at-home mom. I joined mommy groups and hosted play dates; I organized Halloween parties and Christmas cookie recipe-swaps. I presided over the Parent Teacher Association, was team mom for Matthew's football team and assistant leader for Marissa's Girl Scout troop. I did everything my mother had not done for me, and I enjoyed it, I honestly did, but at the same time, something nagged at me. I felt I must be missing something. Was this all there was?

Mark, intent on his work, shrugged aside my restlessness. "Look at what we have," he'd say. "A beautiful family, a comfortable life. What more do you want?" What did I want? I had no idea. At those times, Mark's steady focus lost its appeal, seeming more like stubborn pride, or even deliberate obtuseness, than quiet strength. I stopped complaining, because Mark was right: What did I have to complain about?

I daydreamed sometimes about what my life might have been had I not had children. I could have finished school. I might have pursued an advanced degree. Perhaps, like Naomi, I could have been a writer, or a designer. As a child I had been fascinated with the different colors and textures of things, from the wildflowers growing along the creek to the rough, faded colors of the quilt on the bed I shared with my sister.

But I hadn't done those things, and I'd long ago stopped noticing the soft comfort of my expensive cotton sheets or the rich, earthy colors of the granite countertops in my kitchen. I'd made my choice, with Mark's urging, and instead surrounded myself with durable paints and washable fabrics, kid friendly surfaces that could withstand the test of time, any dreams of a different life shoved to the edges of my consciousness.

I loved my children, but I couldn't help, at times, mourning what I might have been. Because of that, I resented Marissa's glance of disapproval, but I struggled to swallow my irritation. I did not want to fight with her; I'd hoped the trip would bring us closer, but still, I wondered if my devotion to my children, at the expense of myself, had been a mistake. I'd structured my life around Marissa and Matthew. I thought at the very least, I deserved time to relax with a glass of wine.

Chapter 16

Naomi Pritchett Wells

Setting the bottle on the dresser, Beth knelt back down over the suitcase, rooting around for a moment before standing, her face flushed. She held up a corkscrew. "I knew it was in here somewhere," she said, moving beside the bed and reaching for the paper cups stacked atop the nightstand. "Naomi? Will you join me?"

I shook my head. "No, thanks," I said. "I gave up alcohol years ago, about the same time I gave up freeze tag and red rover." I'd meant it to sound humorous, but as my words fell flat into the gulf between us, I realized the absurdity of the situation. It was true; I'd stopped drinking alcohol as soon as I'd been given the choice, at thirteen years of age. I glanced at the clock; it was only half past nine, but for some reason I felt inexplicably tired.

Marissa turned to look at me, her expression a mixture of curiosity and something I couldn't quite define. Amusement, maybe, or even relief. I smiled at her. "You come from a very colorful line, Marissa. I assume your mother has told you about taster duty?"

Marissa shook her head just as Beth answered for her. "No I did *not*, and there's no need to dig up all that old stuff now."

Across the room, Beth's cheeks flamed red as she struggled to open the wine, and I was immediately sorry. "Beth, I hadn't realized. Please forgive me. See? More proof that I would have made a terrible parent. I never do know when to quit talking."

"It's okay," she answered, though it clearly wasn't. "I just haven't seen the point in dwelling on that stuff. Our family had issues; that's no surprise. Let's get this visit over with and get our lives back to normal. Damn it!" She smacked the nightstand in frustration, half the cork on the corkscrew, the other half still wedged in the bottle. "Why do they make these corks so hard to remove?"

Beside me, Marissa stirred, uncrossing her legs and scooting towards the edge of the bed. "You know what, Mom? I'm really tired, and I still have to text Stacey to let her know we made it okay. I think I'm going to go on to my room, if that's okay with you."

Beth waved a dismissive hand. "Sure, honey, that's fine. I'm tired, too, and I still have to call your dad back." She twisted the broken half of the cork from the corkscrew and tossed it in the wastebasket. "Have you told him goodnight?"

Marissa stood, arms crossed over her bare midriff, and nodded. "I just texted him." She smiled a wistful sort of smile. "He told me not to let the bedbugs bite."

Beth grunted, still fighting to remove the broken cork from the bottle, inadvertently pushing it farther down. "Good advice," she said. "Give me a kiss before you go. I'm going to bed soon, myself."

Somewhat gratefully taking my cue, I stood as well. The atmosphere had changed. Gone was the cozy sleepover feeling I'd had just moments before. Instead, the air felt heavy, suffocating; I was reminded of the way I'd felt the day of Luke's funeral, as if I couldn't draw a full breath of air. It crossed my mind that the only times I'd ever felt unable to breathe, I'd been surrounded by Pritchetts.

"I think I'm going to call it a night, too," I told them. "Good night, my niece," I reached out to pat Marissa's shoulder, already fond of the girl, and was both touched and pleased when she put her arms around my neck, pulling me into a hug.

"Good night, my aunt," she responded, and the grief that had lodged in my chest bloomed again, reminding me of all the nights I hadn't had a beautiful niece's arms wrapped around my neck. Aunt Naomi had such a lovely ring to it. I'd missed out on so much without even realizing it.

Marissa released me and I kissed the top of her head before stepping towards Beth and reaching out for an awkward hug. She was still upset, her mouth set in a thin line, and I kicked myself for overstepping my bounds with Marissa. It had never occurred to me that Marissa wouldn't know things about her mother's childhood. "I'm really sorry, Beth," I whispered as I drew her close. "I would never have said anything if I'd known." She squeezed me briefly and stepped away, avoiding my scrutiny.

"It's fine," she said. "I'm just tired, and I don't feel like getting into all that with Marissa tonight." I nodded my understanding and stepped into the hallway, leaving them alone to say their goodnights.

Fifteen minutes later, fresh from a shower in the tiny bath across the hall from the room in which I knew my mother slept, I looked forward to falling into the chenille covered bed that claimed center stage in my cozy room across from Marissa's. Padding softy down the hall towards my room, I was startled to hear Beth, her voice raised, the tone undeniably angry. I hesitated, not sure what to do.

Marissa had still been in her room when I'd left, so my initial assumption was that they were having an argument, no doubt caused by my unfortunate faux pas. I hated that I had created tension between the two of them; Beth had already told me Marissa was going through a rough period. I was torn between going to them to try to soothe the damage I'd done, and worrying that such an action would only make things worse. I had just decided to take my chances and rejoin them when Beth's next words stopped me in my tracks.

"Damn you, Mark, you son of a bitch. How dare you?"

So it wasn't Marissa with whom Beth was fighting. As further validation, just as I turned back towards my room, Marissa's door opened a crack, and I realized she had also heard her mother. She poked her head out long enough to roll her eyes my direction, then shrugged, apparently resigned, and withdrew.

I continued to my room, relieved Beth's quarrel wasn't with Marissa, yet at the same time sorry Marissa had to hear it, and more than a little embarrassed to be witness to a marital argument, or at least, to half of one. I'd been married long enough to know the occasional squabble was unavoidable; Evan and I had certainly had our share of disagreements over the course of our relationship, though I couldn't imagine cursing him, even during the most heated of exchanges. Still, I knew plenty of couples who did. Evan and I no doubt fell on the side of the minority, bookish nerds that we were.

I missed Evan, and hearing the angry words Beth had spoken to her husband made me appreciate my own relationship even more. I thought briefly of calling him, but I knew he'd be asleep. Like me, Evan is an early riser. It's rare for either of us to be awake past ten o'clock in the evening. I knew he wouldn't mind being awakened by the phone, but I didn't want to disturb his rest. Telling myself I'd call him first thing in the morning, I climbed into bed and curled on my side, my back to the window. I could still hear Beth's angry voice from across the hall, the words muffled by the door but the tone still undeniably angry.

I pulled the covers over my head, relishing the comfort of the pillow-topped mattress and the smell of lilac scented sheets. The last time I'd slept in Cedar Hollow, the sheets had smelled of stale sweat, and Beth and I had fought over the dip in the mattress between the rows of metal springs, both of us knowing it was the safest place to sleep if one wanted to avoid being poked during the night. Neither of us had slept well that night. Scenes from Luke's funeral had woven themselves through my dreams: my father standing silent, his head bowed, the muscles of his jaw clenched; my mother, staring straight ahead, her hands clasped tightly in front of her until she stepped forward to sprinkle a handful of dirt into the grave, a grave I found it impossible to believe Luke would inhabit.

His friends from school had stood huddled together, their faces exemplifying the confusion I had felt. Townsfolk had filed by, patting my mother, shaking my father's hand, enveloping Beth and me in sweaty hugs. I reached out for Beth's hand, seeking comfort, but she didn't reach back. Like our mother, Beth had stared straight ahead, lost in her own thoughts. At the end, after the final prayer had been said, my mother climbed into the pickup truck we'd had the entirety of my childhood and waited for my father to drive her home.

I could still see her, just as I had that day when Beth and I climbed into the bed of the truck for the bumpy ride back to Rugged Creek. She had sat perfectly still, unspeaking, her face pale and hard. When we arrived home, she climbed out of the truck and passed through the crowd of people milling about our house without acknowledging their presence. I tried to follow her, needing not only to receive comfort but to give it, but before I could reach her, she stepped into the shadows of her bedroom and closed the door firmly behind her, shutting me out. That was the last time I saw my mother.

I sat up in bed, throwing Erma's chenille spread to the side. The sense of loss was suddenly too great to let me lie down, the air, once again, too heavy for me to breathe.

Chapter 17

Dr. Mark Sloan

The click, followed by a dial tone, sounded sharply against my ear. Beth had hung up on me, certainly not for the first time. I clicked the phone off and set it gently on the counter.

It was getting late; the rooms in the home I'd shared with Beth for twenty-three years had always been notoriously dim. Unlike Beth, I disliked the dark. Whereas she was content to sit for hours in the gloom, staring out at the streetlamps, I obliterated the night at first notice, closing blinds and drawing drapes, walking room to room and turning on lights as I went. The darker the night that pressed against the exterior walls of our home, the more lights I turned on, until no shadows were left to lurk. I wasn't afraid of the dark; rather, I loved the light, with everything exposed exactly as is, no illusions, no misinterpretations.

It hasn't escaped me, throughout our years together, that our preferences for light and dark mimic the essence of who we are. I've always been an open sort of person, a what-you-see-is-what-you-get kind of guy, but much of Beth has always remained secret. Most of Beth, I sometimes suspected, hid behind the very sort of pretense I refused to entertain. The willingness to step out from behind a façade indicates a certain strength, and as time went by, I found myself resenting Beth for not possessing that strength. At the same time, I blamed myself for my inability to help her find it.

Beth is an enigma; it's a part of what first drew me to her. On the one hand, the girl I met in the café was surprisingly naïve, too young and inexperienced to realize the dangers of walking around downtown alone at night, clueless as to the type of monsters lurking in the alleyways. Having been raised in a small town outside of Memphis, I knew the dangers that lurked around the corners. I'd grown into adulthood listening to the disturbing reports of my generation's delinquency on the daily evening news. But Beth seemed incapable, back then, of believing strangers would do her harm simply for the pleasure of it. Her innocence made her endearingly vulnerable at times, too trusting for her own good. From the moment I met her, I felt moved to protect her.

But the other Beth, the one who sat alone in the shadows, was a mystery to me. I knew only the barest of facts regarding her family. It was clear that was an area she didn't wish to discuss, so, after those first heady days, I didn't push her. It's difficult to remember now, but in the beginning I may have thought it curious she never expressed an interest in reconnecting with her family. If so, my curiosity didn't last long. As the only child of only children, I was used to solitude. Within that frame of reference, the disconnect within her family didn't seem as strange to me as it might have to someone else.

It did seem strange, however, that she refused to discuss her childhood. Aside from a couple of romanticized stories of nighttime campouts and ghost stories under the stars, I knew virtually nothing about Beth's past, save the fact that she'd run away to Memphis with her younger sister, and she'd once had a younger brother who had died. Even those things she refused to discuss in detail. I knew, from confessions shared during intimacy in those early days, that her family had a history of moonshining, a tidbit about which I loved to tease her, calling her my moonshine girl. She smiled at my good-natured ribbing but didn't offer more, her silence only adding to the riddle of her past, intriguing me.

I met Naomi only once, shortly after Beth and I started dating, when she came by the café to return some borrowed clothing to Beth. I remember her as a pleasant young woman, pretty in that fresh-faced way Beth always had, but with little to say. She didn't stay long, just handed Beth the bag of clothes, smiled at me and said hello, then left, drawing her hood tightly about her face and hunching her shoulders as she stepped into the cold November rain.

About Luke, the brother, I knew even less. I had no idea how he'd died, and Beth always became so agitated when I brought up the topic that I soon let it drop for good. I assumed the memories caused her pain, something I didn't want to exacerbate. I also assumed she'd eventually share her stories with me, but she never had.

I was drawn to Beth's mystique in the beginning just as much as, and maybe even more than, I was drawn to her innocence. Without a doubt, I enjoyed taking care of her. I'm a caregiver by nature; that's a part of what initially drew me to the field of medicine, but it's only a part.

The fascinating part of practicing medicine, to me, lies in the challenge of correctly identifying symptoms and accurately prescribing a course of treatment. There's a natural high that occurs when the test has been aced, when the treatment takes hold and the patient shows improvement. Once, in a fit of rage, Beth accused me of choosing my career path in order to have my ego consistently stroked, but that wasn't exactly true. I don't crave recognition; accolades from others mean little to me. What drives me is the desire to fit together the pieces of the puzzle.

Thus, I initially found Beth's reticence an intriguing challenge. I wanted to understand her, to unravel the mystery of her hidden past. Beth put up barriers, and I responded to the call to break them down. I'd make this pretty young woman from the mountains feel so safe and protected she'd confide in me her deepest secrets and darkest fears. I would unlock the mystery of Beth.

It didn't work out that way, of course, and remembering the zeal with which I'd thrown myself into the role of rescuer makes me cringe with embarrassment for the narcissistic young man I was. Beth had intuited my penchant for self-aggrandizement, but had erroneously attributed it to the need for external reinforcement. It's true that I never sought praise from colleagues or grateful patients, but what had ever made me think I had the power to banish the demons of someone else?

In spite of my best intentions, I lost her to the shadows somewhere along the way. I've spent countless hours trying to pinpoint exactly when it happened, not that it matters, I suppose, other than as a means of highlighting the point at which I failed her. Or points, rather, since looking back I'm able to identify multiple failings.

I remember vividly one summer afternoon when the children were both still in diapers, Matthew toddling around refusing to potty train, Marissa just learning to crawl. Beth was, understandably, exhausted much of the time, overwhelmed with the responsibility of raising two babies. Unlike many of the couples we knew, Beth and I didn't have relatives to help us. There were no eager grandparents waiting in the wings, listening in anticipation for the phone to ring, jumping at the chance to take the grandkids off our hands and demonstrate their superior parental knowledge. We had no family; indeed, to some extent, we prided ourselves on our independence.

In spite of our pride, the reality was that Beth alone was responsible for raising our children during those early years, and it was not easy for her. I realized this even at the time, but I wasn't sure what to do about it. My clinic was just getting started, demanding my every waking hour and many in which I should have been sleeping. Excited by the apparent success of my practice, I was nevertheless buried under its demands.

Back then, trying to keep our heads above the chaos, Beth never complained about my long hours. In fact, she often sat up late with me, listening to me grumble about the ins and outs of private practice, sharing a glass of wine and commiserating as I picked apart this payer source, that referral entity. But although she didn't complain, I was acutely aware of the unfair burden created by my absence.

On a whim one sunny afternoon, I canceled my afternoon appointments. Maybe it was because, venturing up front to the reception area, I'd had my first glimpse of blue sky that day.

Or maybe it was the breeze blowing in from the Mississippi, reminding me of long summer afternoons spent searching for crayfish—we called them crawdads back then—with friends along the floodplain. More likely, it was the memory of Beth's obvious exhaustion when I left the house that morning, the dark circles under her eyes as she stood holding Matthew on her hip, helping him wave to me as I backed out of the driveway. Whatever the reason, I was suddenly overcome with the urge to surprise her.

Like a giddy schoolboy on his way to a first date, I stopped at a roadside stand and bought her a flower, a long-stemmed red rose encased in plastic wrap. "Hot date?" the scruffy old man at the stand asked me as he counted out my change with grubby fingers, and I shook my head, smiling. "No date," I answered him, "just a very understanding wife."

The old guy paused in his counting and looked up at me from under bushy eyebrows. "Better hold onto her, then," he said, and I agreed.

I felt lucky that day, I remember, my blessings easily counted: two healthy, happy kids, a successful practice, a beautiful new home in a fantastic neighborhood, and a loving, supportive wife. I swung the car into the circular drive and, rose in hand, burst into the house, momentarily blinded by the darkness after the drive through bright sunlight. As I paused, giving my eyes a moment to adjust, I heard a quick movement across the entryway to the right, coming from the kitchen, a burst of water against the porcelain of the sink followed by the soft shutting of a cabinet door.

"Mark! What in the world are you doing home?" I blinked in the dimness and saw Beth heading towards me, wiping her hands on the front of her jeans, leaving wet finger trails down her thighs.

I held the rose toward her, feeling almost shy. "I wanted to surprise you," I said. "I was hoping we could take the kids to the park, maybe have a picnic. What do you think?"

Beth took the rose from my hand and held it to her nose, inhaling deeply. "Delicious," she said, and stood on tiptoe to give me a quick kiss before turning away and going back to the kitchen to rummage through the pantry, eventually pulling out a small vase. It took me a moment to follow her, disconcerted as I was by the unmistakable taste of wine that lingered on my lips after her brief kiss. I'd tasted wine on Beth's lips many times, but never under those circumstances.

I was bothered by that taste, by what it meant. Beth had been home alone with our children, drinking wine at two o'clock in the afternoon. The splash of water when I'd entered the house, the closing of a cabinet door. I was willing to bet if I opened the cabinet where the wine glasses were stored, I'd find one still wet from the hurried rinsing she'd given it upon hearing me enter the house.

"The kids are napping," she said breezily, either unaware of, or pointedly ignoring, my hesitation as she freed the rose from its plastic sleeve and placed it in the vase, filled the vase with water, and set it on the bar, all the while not looking at me. "I really don't want to wake them up; they've been awfully cranky today. But it's so sweet of you to surprise us like this. What do you think about ordering Chinese instead? We can rent a movie and spend an afternoon together right here at home."

In the end, that was what we had done, and it had been an enjoyable evening. I wish we'd had more of them. I didn't mention the wine, not then, and not later. I initially thought I might be overreacting. After all, that was the first time I'd ever known Beth to drink alone. Our times together as a family were so few and far between back then, I didn't want to ruin what little time we had by accusing Beth of something that could have been nothing at all. But of course, it had been something, as I later came to understand.

Sitting alone at the kitchen bar, staring at the phone as if it might magically jump to life and restore Beth's voice to my ear, I reflected on the texts I'd shared earlier with Marissa. Something had to change, that much was clear. Matthew had practically bolted out of our home at the first available opportunity, and Marissa, I feared, was not far behind.

Text-speak aside, Marissa had said: *Dad here we are in this awesome place and it's so beautiful and Aunt Naomi is great. We even went to Peggy's Diner and I met Kay. And then we came back to Vines and Roses to chill for the night but Mom had to bring her wine. I'm going to bed because I don't want to be around her anymore right now, so good night.*

Shortly after that last text, Beth had dutifully called me to say goodnight. Believe it or not, I still felt a little surge of happiness when Beth's name popped up on my caller identification screen. I knew she no longer felt the same, and I wasn't immune to her comments about my long hours and my pretty young receptionist. But the truth was I'd always loved only Beth.

Sometimes it made me angry that as Beth slowly lost sight of who she was, she lost sight of who I am as well. I wasn't a man who took marriage vows lightly, but Beth no longer seemed to know that. In her bid to destroy herself, she was also destroying us: Matthew, Marissa, and me. I refused to allow that to happen to us, but I didn't want it to happen to Beth, either. She needed help; it was time for all of us to admit that, and I wanted to help her, not out of some misguided attempt to play redeemer, but because I loved her.

I had learned more about Beth during the brief moments of our phone call than I'd learned about her throughout our entire marriage, pieces of information that answered some of the many questions I had. Unfortunately, as indicated by the abrupt end to our conversation, she wasn't in a place to accept my help. As much as I loved Beth—had always loved Beth—I couldn't let her destroy us. It was time to make a decision, and I already knew what it had to be.

I stood, more exhausted than I could ever remember feeling, and walked through the house, turning off light after light, my footsteps echoing in the emptiness. I didn't know what the next day would bring, but for that night, the darkness had won.

Chapter 18

Geraldine Porter Pritchett

I see shadows pass by the strip of light under my door and it makes me think of Naomi. She was a sensitive child, always afraid of the dark, hovering outside my door at night when she was just a tiny little thing, trying to work up the courage to knock and ask to crawl in bed with me and Junior for a little while. You'd think sleeping with Beth would have cured her of the nighttime willies, but it never did. Lord knows, Luke didn't help none, always telling the girls stories about escaped murderers hiding in the woods, or convincing them Sasquatch was lurking under the porch waiting to grab their ankles.

He did love to get them worked up, that boy did. They'd lay up there on the roof when the floods came, squealing and carrying on until finally Junior'd get fed up and grab the broom, jumping up on the bed in his boxers to pound it against the ceiling, hollering at them to hush up and let a body get some rest. They'd quiet down for a little while, but never for long.

What a rascal my Luke was. I can still see him smiling at me with his crooked smile like it was only yesterday. Even now, it boggles my mind how a family can go from all that noise, all that hollering and carrying on, to nothing but silence, just like that. One day I had a family, and the next day, I did not.

I reckon I've had ample time to blame near about everybody for my children leaving me. I blamed Valerie Poindexter for not stopping the girls before they got to the station, I blamed the stationmaster for believing the girls and letting them get on that train, and I blamed the conductor for taking them away from me. I blamed my momma and my daddy for holding onto me so tight when I was a child that I didn't hold onto my own children tight enough, and they slipped away. I blamed Junior for everything rotten about his family and everyone else's, and I blamed myself for my weaknesses, too many to count, starting with loving Junior and allowing him to give me children who would cause me nothing but pain. I even blamed Luke himself for dying.

Momma, Daddy, Luke, and then Junior, they're all gone now, away from any blame I can lay on them. The only ones left are me and the girls, and I'll tell you the truth, I've laid a heavy burden of blame on them for many a year, for leaving me like they did. Them coming back after all this time has wrought havoc on my mind, and I don't know what to think.

Some nights after they was all gone and it was just me and Junior laying in bed, him snoring, and me tossing and turning, trying to find some peace, I'd dream about Naomi. The Naomi in my dreams wasn't the almost grown up girl who ran away from me, it was the baby girl who used to come looking for me in the night. I'd hear the creak of her door, and then the soft whispery sound of her little feet against the rough floorboards of the hallway. I'd feel her standing outside my door, her presence just as real to me as Junior was, with his big old heavy leg thrown over my thighs while he slept.

I'd lay there half awake and half asleep and wait for that tiny knock at my door, so quiet I couldn't hardly hear it, wishing she'd hurry up and come on in so I could pull her soft little body up next to me and go back to sleep. But always, sometime while I was laying there, waiting on that knock, it would hit me just as hard as it did when I first found out they'd gotten on that train: my children was gone. Naomi wasn't at my door; wasn't nobody there anymore except me and Junior.

I have come to believe there ain't nothing hurts worse than waking up again to the world you was finally able to escape in your sleep, having to know again all the things you was able to forget in your dreams. In some ways it seems to me like the second knowing is even harder than the first, because you wake up feeling lucky, like there might be some hope in the day, and then you remember there ain't no hope at all.

I am dreaming of my baby Naomi again, my little Nay-nay, but I know by now, even in my sleep, that she ain't real. I see the shadow feet under the door, and I hear the soft knock. I hear her saying, "Momma," like she always used to say, but I won't be fooled this time. This is what I am telling myself, but the knock comes again, a little louder, and then the voice, "Momma." And my heart jumps into my throat because I know the voice, but at the same time I don't know it at all. It is my Naomi but different, and before I know what I am doing, I am throwing back the covers and swinging my legs off the side, moving faster than I have moved this entire last month since I took to my bed.

"Naomi," I answer her, and I still can't quite believe this is real. "Naomi." I am expecting to wake up like I have for the last twenty-seven years, to silence and a weight on my chest. "I'm comin', baby girl," I say, and my voice is rusty because I haven't spoken for so long. "I'm comin'." *Wait for me oh don't leave don't leave don't leave.* How could I have ever feared feeling nothing for these children? I realize now that I've been waiting lifetimes just to hear that baby call for me again.

Chapter 19

Beth Pritchett Sloan

After a sleepless night, I was relieved to see the first light of dawn making its way into my east facing room, bringing the antique furnishings out of the shadows. I'd had a terrible night, upset not only by my fight with Mark, but also dreading the upcoming confrontation with my mother, for that's how I'd come to think of it—not so much a visit as a confrontation. Pushing aside the tangled sheets, I scrubbed my face with my hands, exhausted, before stepping onto the polished wood floor of Vines and Roses and nearly sliding down as my foot landed on my cell phone.

Frustrated nearly beyond endurance, I'd thrown it onto the bed the night before, after hanging up on Mark, where it had bounced and clattered to the floor. I had known coming back to Cedar Hollow was a mistake, and with every passing minute, that knowledge had been reinforced. I picked up the cell and tossed it onto the bed once again, then stumbled to the window to throw back the curtains, eager, for once, for the light of day.

In spite of my dark mood, I couldn't deny the beauty of the sunrise, the colors stretched across the sky above the dark backdrop of mountains. A wispy haze hung across the valley, and dew still sparkled on the grass. Somewhere in the distance a mourning dove called, the solitary notes hanging in the still air. In another few minutes the haze would be gone, replaced by the sultry humidity of a West Virginia summer, but for a moment I was transported back in time, running barefoot through the wet grass on a cool summer morning, with Naomi on one side and Luke flying ahead, fishing poles bouncing on his shoulder.

The memory of that morning was so real I could feel the misty air against my face; it smelled of the damp leaves we trampled underfoot, and of the brook trout Luke pulled proudly from the creek. "It's at least ten inches," he was saying, holding it up for our inspection. "At least. Don't you think?"

I had laughed. "Eight, maybe," I told him. "If you're lucky." Looking at the colorful fish, I had to admit it was the biggest brook trout I'd ever seen, the greenish blue sides fading into a belly so pink it was almost scarlet.

"Let it go, Luke," Naomi said, reaching out a finger to stroke the fish's head. At her touch, the trout jerked against the line Luke had threaded through its gill slit, and Naomi jumped. "Please let it go," she begged. "We don't need it, Luke."

"What do you mean we don't need it?" Luke stared at her, disbelieving. "We're fishing Naomi. This is what people do when they go fishing. They catch fish, and this one's a beauty. There's no way I'm turning it loose." He secured the line around a sapling on the bank and lowered the tethered fish to the water for safekeeping, hoping, no doubt, to add many more to the line before the morning was over.

Naomi squatted on the bank, gazing into the water where the fish continued to thrash against the line. "Luke," she said looking up at him, tears brimming. "Please. You're hurting it."

Luke paused, his hand in the carton of worms. "Naomi, you can't be serious."

I watched the two of them, not invested enough in either point of view to intervene, curious as to what the outcome would be. After what seemed an eternity, Luke shook his head and snorted with disgust.

"Fine, Naomi. Let it go." He tossed the carton of bait beside her on the ground where it spilled, the dark soil covering her bare feet as the worms scrambled for cover. "Let them go, too, why don't you. Lord knows, I wouldn't want to hurt a worm. And next time I go fishing, you are *not* coming with me. Got it?"

Shooting Naomi one last scathing look, Luke stomped off down the trail, headed the opposite direction from home. Standing at the window of Vines and Roses nearly three decades later, I could still see him, his bare back tanned, his body rigid with anger as he wiped the mud from his hands on the worn seat of his cut-off denim shorts. Luke was a handsome boy, with the dark, curly hair of the Pritchetts and the gangly height of the Porters. Though he was the youngest of the three of us, he already towered over Naomi and me. His recent growth spurt left him clumsy, not quite used to his own body, and I couldn't help but be amused as I watched his angry progression through the woods.

Squatting on the ground beside me, Naomi wasted no time freeing the fish from its line, grinning the whole time, not in the least bothered by Luke's anger. "Beth," she'd said as she struggled with the fish, "hurry up and put those worms in the shade, would you? If you don't, they'll burn up. Careful not to step on them."

We didn't see Luke again until dinner, and even then he refused to speak to Naomi, no matter how hard she tried to tickle and hug him into a more forgiving mood. He was a good brother, our Luke. He had wanted that trout, but not enough to cause Naomi tears. By the next morning his anger had dissipated, as we had known it would, and he was back to teasing Naomi, clucking like a chicken when she scooped up a bite of eggs, grunting, pig-like, when she munched on a piece of bacon. We had no way of knowing, as we laughed together that sunny morning, that we would soon lose Luke.

Naomi and I could not have guessed that within a few short weeks, we would leave Cedar Hollow and not return for another twenty-seven years. I wondered what we might have changed, had we known. Standing at my window in the hush of early morning, knowing what became of us all, I felt a heartrending sadness for the children in my memory. I had not wanted to return to Cedar Hollow, had, in fact, been desperately afraid of all that awaited me there. But I needed to make peace with Luke. I didn't know how I could, but I knew I had to try. Everything else depended on that.

Movement on the street in front of me caught my attention, drawing me from my memories. Glancing down, I saw a car, some sort of older model sedan, pulling into the lot of Peggy's Diner across and to the left of the boarding home. As I watched, the door swung open and Kay stepped slowly out, pulling herself up on the frame. She pushed the door closed and rummaged in her oversized purse for a moment before letting herself into the service door at the back of the restaurant.

I checked my watch; it was barely six a.m. The boarding home was quiet around me, with no signs of life. I knew what I needed to do, had known from the beginning, since receiving Kay's letter in the mail, though I hadn't wanted to acknowledge it. First, though, I'd visit Kay, not only for coffee, but for strength, almost as if providence had led me to her. Bypassing the shower, I dressed quickly, washed my face and brushed my teeth, then quietly let myself out of the boarding home, taking care not to wake the sleeping souls around me.

From somewhere long past, possibly from something Mark had once told me, a quote insinuated itself into my thoughts. Charles Dederich, a reformed alcoholic who founded a drug rehabilitation center in the 1950s, is often credited with coining the phrase *today is the first day of the rest of your life*. No phrase seemed more apt as I walked into the damp West Virginia morning, the haze burning off overhead as the sun finally conquered the mountains.

Chapter 20

Marissa Elizabeth Sloan

I didn't know what the sound was that woke me up; I'd never heard anything like it. At first it was in my dream. I was dancing, practicing the latest routine with Stacey, a quick jazz number with a rocking bongo solo, when all of a sudden she dropped to the floor and started crying, but she didn't have any tears. She was just sort of moaning or something, a sad sound, the saddest sound I'd ever heard.

I was upset, because Stacey *never* cries. She's like the most cheerful person I know. I'm the one who cries about everything, and Stacey is the one who teases me about it. I thought maybe she'd hurt herself, maybe twisted her ankle or pulled a muscle doing a pivot step, so I ran over to her and knelt down to see what was wrong, and that's when the dream just—*poof*—disappeared, and I realized I was in my bed, except that it wasn't my bed. My bed was littered with journals, books, hairbands, and clothes. This bed was full and soft and smelled like flowers, like the lilac scented spray I'd gotten for Christmas one year when my mother finally realized I was old enough for perfume.

And then there was that sound again, and just hearing it made me feel lonely. In some ways, it sounded like an owl, or at least like owls sounded in movies and on T.V. I'd never actually heard a real owl. I pushed back the covers and sat up, confused for a second when, instead of a poster of Bruno Mars (my favorite singer ever, and oh my God those *eyes*!), I found myself staring across the room at my own face, reflected back at me in the dim light from a big, heavy mirror attached to what my mother had said was an antique washstand.

That's when I remembered where I was. I was so excited I jumped straight out of bed and headed for the window to see if I could figure out what was making that lonesome sound. Underneath the lacy curtains the window had one of those old style window shades, the kind you have to pull down a little bit to make it roll up, and it took me a minute to get it to work, but when I did ... wow. It was like looking into a painting, something by one of those famous old guys I learned about when my mom signed me up for art classes, like Renoir or Monet or someone. It was beautiful.

In the distance, the sky over the mountains was red and pink and purple, and the mountains looked almost black underneath. As I watched, the sun rose over them, lighting up the town right in front of my eyes. Up close, below my window, the yard of the boarding home was full of flowering bushes, rhododendrons, I think, like the ones my friend Jamie's mom used to have before she got too sick to take care of them.

They were planted on both sides of the front walk, around the trees, all along the front of the house, and they were the same colors as the sunrise, coral, light pink, purple, and red. For some reason, I hadn't noticed them the day before, maybe because I was so caught up in getting to know Aunt Naomi. But now they were impossible to miss, and all of a sudden I wanted more than anything to breathe in the fresh air. I just knew it would be different from what I was used to.

I worried the window might be hard to open, but it wasn't. It slid right up, and I leaned forward trying to see everything all at once, and then I heard that sad call again, coming from a huge tree over to my left. It was obviously some kind of bird, and I wondered if it always sounded that way, or if it was just having a really bad morning. I kept looking, trying to get a glimpse of it, wondering if it looked as mysterious as it sounded. Besides the bird, there were no other sounds until I heard what sounded like a footstep, like a shoe on pavement, and I leaned out farther to get a look.

It was my mom. While I watched, she turned left off the front walk and started down the street towards the center of town. I almost called out to her, but stopped myself. If she'd wanted me to go with her, she would have asked. Maybe, like me, she had wanted to breathe the fresh air, but she didn't walk like that was what she was doing. She was walking fast, like she was late for an appointment or something. I had definitely not been expecting to see her up and out this early. My mother was known for sleeping late; she was hardly ever up early enough to see me off to school.

While I watched, she walked up to Peggy's Diner and knocked on the door, not the front door, but the back one. After a few seconds the door opened and she went inside. What in the world was she doing? And why would she have left me at the boarding home without her the very day I was supposed to meet my grandmother? I didn't want to be angry with her, I really didn't, but I couldn't help it.

I slammed the window shut a little harder than I'd meant to, and turned to get dressed. I'd go find Aunt Naomi and ask her what was going on. Thank God I'd finally met someone else in my family who seemed relatively normal. Quite frankly, I was getting tired of being the only one.

Chapter 21

Naomi Pritchett Wells

As the dawning sky turned from black to gray, I sat in the soft glow of lamplight across from my mother and poured us both a cup of coffee. I don't know how Erma had known to find me in my mother's room, but she had, knocking gently at the door and calling me by name. "I thought you ladies might need this," she'd said, holding a steaming pot of coffee in one hand, a basket of mugs and spoons, sugar and cream in the other. And indeed, we did.

My eyes burned from lack of sleep, but it scarcely mattered. As my mother had said when I urged her to rest, "I spent all them years you was gone sleepin'. There ain't no time for that now."

I settled back in the wingchair across from her and spread the afghan she handed me across my lap. She was right; there would be plenty of time for sleep later. We had catching up to do, and I think some small part of me was afraid if I left her room, I'd lose her once again.

I had not known what to expect when I knocked on my mother's door in the middle of the night. As I approached, trying to be as stealthy as my stiff, popping joints would allow after a long day of travel, I had realized forty-two wasn't really that much different from two in that regard. I'd never known what to expect when I approached my mother's door in the dark of night. I'd always been afraid of her anger, which could be fierce, though in truth I don't remember her ever turning me away on the nights I craved her comfort.

Therein lies the crux of everything. Sometimes, there'd been no basis for my fear, but other times, there was no warning of her anger—an impossible minefield for a child to successfully maneuver. An innocent action that might one day draw a smile could the next day draw a slap, depending on my mother's mood. In spite of that, I did believe she loved us; I'd always believed in my mother's love. What I hadn't believed in was her ability to show it in a way that wouldn't hurt me—or indeed, to show it at all.

Once, in an attempt to better understand my family history, Evan had asked me to describe my mother. Until then, I'd never attempted to place parameters around the memory of my mother, and somewhat to my dismay, I'd found I couldn't. She had always been a mystery to me. I think, looking back with the perspective of age, my mother had been torn between the life she'd been raised to live, and the life she had chosen on her own.

She had loved my father beyond reason; of that there is no doubt. As children, we all knew my father came first. There were times we resented that fact, times we struggled with knowing no matter how much we needed her to interfere, she would not. He could strike us in anger, dribble whiskey down our throats, ridicule us into obscurity—my mother would not intervene.

At times like those, when we implored her to help us, she, too, could strike out with little provocation. I think she simply didn't know how to love our father and protect us at the same time. Her marriage to my father had been a rebellion against her own parents. If she betrayed him, she betrayed herself. When she had to choose between her husband and her children, her husband had to win; otherwise, she had lost.

And yet there were also times when she laughed at our jokes, smiled at our accomplishments, and pulled us close. Once, when she was ill with the flu, she asked me to sit with her and keep her company. I sat in a chair by the foot of the bed and watched her as she dozed. I must have been around ten years old at the time, and I was ecstatic my mother wanted me near her. I sat with her until she awakened and sent me away, telling me I'd wasted enough of my day watching her sleep.

I have a vivid memory of my mother teaching Beth and me to make clover chains, tying the stems of the furry flowers together until she adorned us with crowns and necklaces. It was also my mother who taught us to collect fireflies—we called them lightning bugs—in a jar on warm summer nights. I remember her standing on the porch, smiling at the three of us as we explored the dark woods with our homemade lanterns, eager to establish our own Mecklenburg.

My mother could surprise us, too, though rarely. One Easter weekend, after she'd spent time in Kentucky visiting an elderly aunt, she brought us chocolate. I remember it clearly, because we didn't celebrate Easter. I had never participated in an egg hunt, nor had I ever been presented with a basket. We sat on the porch, Beth, Luke and I, waiting for our father to bring her home. We were anxious to see her. In spite of whatever resentments we may have already been hoarding, she was our mother, and we missed her. When they finally arrived and she stepped out of the truck, smiling, and handed each of us a chocolate Easter bunny, I was beside myself with excitement. I hugged her so hard she gasped.

"Careful, Naomi, you'll squeeze the life out of me."

Even my father had smiled. I had expected him to become angry. He didn't like it when my mother spent money, particularly on something as frivolous as candy. He hadn't, though. He seemed particularly solicitous of our mother that weekend, and I realized he, too, must have missed her.

Those peaceful instances were woefully few and far between, but when they occurred, were magical. I later realized those happy instances with our mother were only a part of our lives when all was well with my father. He received the majority of our mother's energy, and we received whatever was left. My father demanded a lot. Rarely did she have the reserves required to engage us. As a child I recognized this, although I could not have put it into words.

My mother loved me, no doubt, but I knew in the deepest recesses of my heart she didn't love me as much as I needed her to, and this hurt me deeply. What I now understand, but didn't then, is that the amount of love she gave us wasn't based on anything we did or didn't do; rather, it was based on her own mental state. In some ways, my mother was not well, and as her children, we paid the price.

Creeping down the dark hallway of the boarding home, hoping I'd come across neither family nor stranger, I had felt a mixture of fear and anticipation that, although I hadn't felt it in decades, was still familiar. As I had so often as a child, I stopped, nearly turning back to my own room before ultimately gambling that she'd be too old, or too tired, to erect the wall she had sometimes planted between us.

I hesitated before knocking, wondering which mother would answer: the one who, in the best of times, had loved nothing more than to splash alongside her children in Rugged Creek, or the one who watched her children struggle against the restraining hands of her husband without stepping forward to rescue them.

As it turned out, it was neither. I did not recognize the woman who opened the door to me. In my memory, my mother was tall and commanding and very beautiful. This woman was stooped, her face gaunt and lined with deep creases, her white hair thin and wispy. She peered up at me, squinting in the light from the hallway with an expression unfamiliar to me. It wasn't the anger I had dreaded, or the dismissal I had expected. It was something I had never before seen in my mother's eyes: a desperate hope. Before I could react, she wrapped her arms around me. I returned her embrace and we stood for several long seconds without speaking, my mother crying quietly against my shoulder.

In the beginning we were cautious with one another, circling carefully as she stepped aside and invited me in, standing awkwardly as she hurriedly buttoned up her robe and fumbled with a bedside lamp before finding the switch and bathing the room in muted light. Finally, she motioned me towards a matching set of wingchairs and I sat, pulling a plush yellow throw pillow against my stomach, gripping it tightly as if might afford some sort of protection.

During those first tense moments, I nearly regretted my decision. Had I waited until morning, I would have at least been afforded the distraction of Beth and Marissa. As it was, the void of our missing years stretched only between the two of us.

I found myself without words. I had no idea where to begin, so I waited for what seemed an eternity for my mother to settle herself across from me. Under her steady gaze I fidgeted with the pillow, smoothing the nubby fabric with clammy hands until she leaned forward, her own hands quietly clasped in her lap.

"Naomi," she said, and I started; it was strange, hearing my mother call my name. Even as a child she had rarely called me by name, preferring Nay-nay, the nickname a young Luke had given me when my given name proved too difficult to pronounce.

"Naomi," she said again. "Where have you been?" This not in an accusatory tone, but rather as if, instead of having been absent from her for the majority of my life, I'd simply returned late from an errand, perhaps a trip to Mr. Smith's General Store. "Where have you been, child?" She tilted her head to the side, her expression questioning, the tear tracks still visible on her cheeks reflecting the glow from the lamp.

So I told her, about the train ride, the garage apartment, the café, and later about the bookstore and the writing classes. I told her about Evan and my fantasy series, about the many rejections and the trials and triumphs of a writing career. I even told her about Shiva, about how he sits on the windowsill of my office, switching his tail from side to side while I struggle with plots and protagonists and sentence structure. "He's sort of like my muse," I said, wincing with embarrassment as I said it, but she only nodded, her eyes never leaving mine.

As I talked, she listened, hardly moving, asking an occasional question, making an infrequent comment. We avoided the hard topics. That would come in time.

Only once did the conversation falter. Just before Erma brought us coffee, my mother had asked about Beth. I was unable to fill in many of the gaps in Beth's life because I didn't know them myself. I think this surprised my mother. I suppose she had assumed we'd been together all that time. Upon learning the truth, she looked down at her lap, the first time she'd looked away from me since finding me at her door, and shook her head once, her mouth working in silence. Then she spoke a phrase I knew well. "Blossoms are scattered by the wind, and the wind cares nothin' ..."

It was my turn to look surprised, and I almost answered her, responding with *but the blossoms of the heart no wind can touch*, the poignant conclusion to her quote, but I thought I must surely have misheard her. As a writer, I was familiar with the works of Yoshida Kenkō, but how could my mother, a woman who'd spent her entire life in Cedar Hollow, West Virginia, possibly know the poetry of a Japanese monk who'd been dead for centuries? Before I could ask, Erma had knocked on the door with coffee.

I'd just settled back in my chair, the afghan snugly around me, when my mother spoke again. "I reckon there's more to all of us than others realize," she said, and I felt my face flush with embarrassment. How presumptuous of me to have made assumptions about my mother when I knew virtually nothing about her. The sense of loss I'd felt earlier bloomed in my chest, and I set my coffee cup down, the aroma no longer enticing.

"Where do you think you might have got your love of books from, Naomi?" Her voice was chiding, her smile rueful. "I wasn't never the smartest child in school." She waved towards me as I started to protest, motioning me to listen. "It's true; I wasn't, but a few things have stuck with me, in spite of it. I loved to read, and even if I hadn't, I didn't have no choice about it. My momma saw to that."

If I knew little about my mother, I knew even less about my grandmother. My grandparents both passed away before Luke was born, and I have no real memories of either of them. I don't recall my mother ever speaking of her parents, and we were surrounded by so many Pritchetts as children I don't think it ever occurred to us to ask about the Porters. How sad, I thought, that we never asked about her family. The longer I sat with her, the more I found myself wanting to know Geraldine Porter Pritchett, not the woman I remembered as my mother, but the woman beyond that.

She shifted in her chair, rearranging the robe over her thin legs, pushing a pillow farther behind her back. Although we'd talked for hours by that time, her physical condition continued to alarm me. Her legs were blue veined and bruised beneath the robe, and she moved slowly, as if it pained her to change positions. I had always seen my mother as invincible, but I was quickly learning that my memories of my mother were not an accurate indication of who she was.

"Now tell me about Marissa," she said, changing the subject before it became too much. "Is she as smart as you girls always was?"

Grateful for the redirection, I was doing as she'd requested and telling her everything I'd come to know about Marissa when we were once again interrupted by a knock at the door.

Chapter 22

Kay Langley

I don't care what people say, there is a knowing some folks have, and I have always been one of them folks. Laugh if you will, but it's the truth. Just as sure as I knew the sun was going to come up, I knew Beth Pritchett was going to come looking for me. Believe what you want, but I knew.

That's how I come to be at the diner so early on a Friday morning, a day when I'd usually be sleeping in a little, taking a little rest, as Andrew always says. Riva opens on Fridays, but I'd been taking stock of things long enough to know I'd be needed that morning, so I was ready with coffee when Beth showed up at my door.

It was clear she hadn't had a restful night. Her hair was a mess, stuck up all over her head like she hadn't taken time to comb it, her face was pale and tired, and her blouse was rumpled. I sat her down at the table we keep back in the kitchen for family and poured her a cup of coffee. She tried to wave away the breakfast I fixed her, just a light meal of toast and fruit, but I set it in front of her anyway. "Whatever it is, starvin' yourself won't fix it," I told her, spearing a strawberry off my own plate.

It took a while before she started to talk, but I waited her out. One thing I have learned, living my life in this diner, is if you keep quiet and wait long enough, people will talk. It has often struck me that one of the things wrong with this world is that people aren't willing to sit quiet and wait. We like to fill up all the spaces with noise, but we can learn a whole lot more by sitting quiet. Sure enough, before I'd gotten halfway through my toast, Beth began to talk.

I listened all the way through, handing her tissues when she needed them and refilling her coffee cup when it ran empty. When she finally got it all out, all the words and the tears, she held her face in her hands, plumb exhausted from the telling. That's when I spoke.

"Beth," I told her, "you said you didn't know what to do, but that ain't quite true. You know what you need to do; you just ain't yet made up your mind to do it."

She sat quiet for a bit before she pushed herself back in the chair, scrubbing her face so hard with her palms I was afraid she'd put out an eye. "I know, Kay," she said. "I know. You're right, and I will do it, although for the life of me, I can't imagine how. But first, I need to talk to Luke."

I nodded. That was surely the place to start, and I was glad she saw it that way, too. "Well, honey," I told her, "I imagine you know where to find him."

"I do," she said, "but I'm afraid to go back there. Not just to the bridge, but to our house. Is it even still there?"

I nodded again. "The house is there, all right," I told her. But there ain't nobody at it now. Your momma was the last one to leave."

Beth snorted. "How'd she manage to get rid of all the Pritchetts in the yard? God knows, I wish she'd gotten rid of them when we still lived there. Did they leave when Daddy died?"

"They've been gone a long time, Beth," I told her. "They pretty much left of their own accord, not too long after Luke passed and you and Naomi left." She looked surprised to hear that, and I was a little bit amused. "Did you think they was still back there, runnin' shine like in the old days?"

"I guess I picture it pretty much as I left it," she answered. "It's hard for me to imagine it any differently."

I patted her hand. "Honey, the 'shine business dried up years before your daddy finally let it go. Oh, they had a couple of customers who hung on with the changin' times, people who couldn't be bothered to drive to Huntington for the hard stuff they craved, but Pritchetts hadn't made a livin' selling whiskey since before Old Man Pritchett died. Hell, honey, you know as well as I do the stills was more for personal consumption than anythin' else. As far as I know, your daddy didn't give no explanation for quittin', not that he'd have given it to me, anyway. Next thing any of us in town knew, his brothers all kind of scattered away, leavin' him and your momma alone up by the creek. And that's where they stayed, 'til he passed on last year."

Beth pondered on that for a minute. "Did he stop drinking?" she asked. "I can't imagine an absence of alcohol at that house. Whiskey was at the center of everything."

"Now that I don't know," I told her. "I can tell you I never saw Junior drunk here in town, but then again, I never really saw Junior in town. He kept to himself, you know, like he always had. But what I can tell you is if it's drunken relatives you're afraid of, there ain't none of them up there now."

"I have to admit," she said, standing and smoothing her blouse, "I was a little afraid of that. But I can't define what it is I'm really afraid of. Ghosts, maybe, or memories. Both, I guess. Nevertheless, it's time for me to do this—past time, really." She took a deep breath and squared her shoulders.

I walked her to the door and she hugged me before stepping out into a morning that was shaping up to be just fine. I watched her walk away from me, her shoulders hunched up again, her head down, but heading forward just the same. Folks was starting to move about. Valerie Poindexter waved at me from the front of the library down past the boarding home, and Corinne Johnson honked as she drove by, the white bun of hair on top of her head barely showing above the steering wheel.

Corinne was headed the same direction Beth had gone on foot, and I figured she must be going up to Crutcher Mountain to help out at the children's lodge. The kids would be leaving today, and Corinne had taken to helping Opal Huffman, the housekeeper, with organizing the brunch and tour the staff always provided for the parents and caseworkers on the last day.

Thinking on the Huffmans reminded me I needed to get an apple pie going. Richard and Opal liked to stop by for a slice on Friday afternoons, and I imagined Corinne might stop in along with them, and maybe Jessie, too. Friday afternoons could get crowded in my diner. I needed to get busy.

I glanced one last time down the street, towards the boarding home over on the right, and saw that Erma already had the curtains and blinds thrown open to the new day. Beth wouldn't be there when Geraldine woke up, but that was all right about that. She needed to get her business settled with the dead before she could settle it with the living.

Tires crunched on gravel and I turned to see Riva pulling in, with Dennis Lane and his daddy Darryl right behind her in Dennis' big old truck. They'd be wanting their breakfast before opening up the store. The Lanes ate breakfast with me near about every morning, had since Darryl's wife had passed on a couple of years ago. I think it filled up a hole in their lives, to tell you the truth, having a routine. I know it filled up a hole in mine. After a lifetime of scrambling to get food on the table for a hungry family, there's something sad about eating breakfast alone.

It looked to be just an ordinary morning in Cedar Hollow, with folks going about their business the way they always do. But I knew there wasn't nothing ordinary about our little town. I stepped back into the diner, pulling the service door shut behind me, and went to switch the *Closed* sign to *Open*, wondering about all the things that was bound to happen before I switched it back to *Closed*.

Chapter 23

Geraldine Porter Pritchett

"Aunt Naomi," the child's voice calls through the door, and Naomi throws the afghan aside and jumps to her feet to let the girl in, looking at me first to make sure it's all right. Of course it's all right; I know who this child must be, so I nod and gesture at the door, but even if it ain't all right I don't think I have enough of my wits about me to say so. I am still trying to get it set in my mind that this sophisticated woman I've been talking to all this time is my Naomi. Some crazy part of me finds pride in the fact that she's grown up so well, but that's stupid, ain't it? She was still a child when she left. I haven't had a goddamned thing to do with her growing up.

I do remember that Naomi was sophisticated even as a little thing. I don't mean sophisticated in a I'm-better-than-you kind of way, I mean sophisticated in a I'm-comfortable-in-my-own-skin kind of way. She just always knew what she wanted and what she didn't, soon as she was old enough to walk, or maybe even before. I always admired that in my Naomi, even if sometimes I envied it. Well, that's the truth.

As I remember now, Naomi made it known real clear within that first week or two that she didn't want my milk. There wasn't no mistaking that, with her little face all red, screwed up in a holler. I wasn't too happy about it, but there wasn't nothing I could do. The baby had to eat, whether she liked me or not.

I sent Junior to get me some formula to feed her instead, thankful Mr. Smith had some down at the store. Right away I felt a little bit like I'd failed her, but that feeling didn't last long. Naomi was quick to make it known she wanted me, following me all around the house with her eyes as a baby, toddling after me as soon as she could walk, and knocking on my door at night when she moved out of her crib. Sometimes Naomi wanted me so much I wished she would reject me, even if just for a little while, it could wear on me so.

Yes, I seen quick enough she wasn't rejecting me with her refusal of my milk; she was just making her stand. She didn't like it, so she wouldn't have it. I couldn't fault her for that, even as I wondered where she found her strength. She was a tough one, my Naomi.

I remember one time when she was barely even old enough to talk, when Junior was teasing her, holding her blanket just out of where she could reach it. She loved that raggedy old blanket, she did. I don't even know who it had belonged to first, having made its way all through Junior's family. It was faded to what might have been a light pink, or maybe it had at one time been white and something red faded on it; it was impossible to tell. The tacking was coming off around the edges and moths had eaten holes in the middle of it, but Naomi didn't care. That blanket went everywhere with her, drug on the ground behind her when she toddled around the yard.

Anyway, for whatever reason—maybe the corn was looking good or he'd gotten a new order—that particular day Junior was in a playful mood. Most days, when the babies was too young to work, he didn't pay no attention to them at all, other than to holler at me to stop their crying. But every so often, he'd seem to sort of notice them, and when he did, they amused him to no end if they was in a good place at that time. If they wasn't … well, there ain't no point in thinking on that at this late date. The past is the past.

On that particular day he was tickled, and what tickled him was Naomi's determination to get that blanket away from him. He kept at it for the longest time, holding it out to her, pulling it away just as she managed to grab hold of it, all the while laughing as if he'd plumb lost whatever good sense God had seen fit to give him. Then, after about the fourth or fifth time Junior had tricked her that way, yanking the blanket away from her little hands, Naomi did the most peculiar thing.

She stood there, such a little thing, her face and bare chest filthy, her dark hair long and tangled all about her head, swaying back and forth in her big old plastic diaper pants, and looked her daddy square in the eye. Then she shrugged her bony little shoulders, her not even old enough to know what such a thing meant, and turned around with her bare back to Junior and walked right out the front door, diaper hanging between her knees, barely old enough to even keep her balance, leaving him holding that raggedy blanket all by himself.

I couldn't help myself but to laugh, thinking, there you go, my little baby girl, give back as good as you get. And I reckon she did, too. Junior sat there and sputtered for a minute before throwing Naomi's blanket into the fire, but that's a whole other story I don't have the strength to tell today.

Now, with the knocking at the door, Naomi jumps up and undoes the lock. The sight of that beautiful girl standing in the doorway, looking so much like her momma had the last time I'd seen her, plumb takes my breath away. I struggle to get up on my swollen feet, grabbing hold of the arms of my chair to boost myself off, but before I can get my feet under me, the girl sees me.

"Aunt Naomi, my mom left," she starts to say, and then, "Oh!"

She pushes past Naomi, crossing the room to kneel down at my feet. I let go the arms of my chair, dropping back down with a sense of relief. It's hard getting up these days, particularly since I ain't in the best of health. Deciding to die has taken its toll on me, a fact that is starting to annoy the hell out of me now that it looks like I am bound to live. I don't know whether to cuss Kay or to thank her, but I'll have to figure that out later. Right now, to my amazement, the pretty young girl at my knees is reaching to hug my neck.

"You're my grandmother," she says, "and I'm Marissa, Beth's daughter. What should I call you? Grandma?"

It takes me a minute to get my arms to hug her back, not because I don't want to—Lord knows I want to, so bad I can feel myself trembling—but because I ain't had nobody come at me with a hug in longer than I can remember. My body don't remember how to respond to someone else's touch. Even Naomi, at my door earlier, didn't come at me with a hug, though she did put her arms around me when I leaned against her.

We wasn't never a touchy sort of family. Junior didn't cater to shows of weakness, and I catered to Junior. Sure, I know that. When you get old, you ain't got much choice except to admit how you got to where you're at. My love for Junior overtook my own good sense, and don't think I haven't lost sleep over that fact. But in the end, Junior was the only one left to me, wasn't he? Some nights, when I can't sleep, I recognize at some point I made a choice, but I am afraid to wonder if it was the right one.

Now this sweet child is hugging my neck while Naomi looks on, and I am hugging her back, surprising myself with the wetness on my cheeks. Twice now I have cried these last few hours, and that's more than I've cried since they pulled my Luke from that confounded creek. Since Kay has decided I need to live, there is a whole different life put before me. I'm not sure what to make of it; my mind is pulled in so many directions. But there is one thing I'm sure of, and that is that this sweet child should call me Nana. It's the name I dreamed about during all those years of watching the women in town with their grandbabies, wishing I had a grandbaby of my own. Now I do.

I know one more thing, too: Beth ain't here. That hurts my heart some, and I reckon whatever it was made her run away from me all them years ago is still making her run. I find myself needing to know why that is, while at the same time wanting to hide from the knowing.

Chapter 24

Naomi Pritchett Wells

As children, we'd worn a path from our house into town so completely onto the bank of Rugged Creek it was nearly a ditch, packed hard and trampled down by years of our running, skipping, strolling feet. I could have traversed it in the dark, and had, on moonlit nights when Luke and I were feeling sufficiently daring. As far as I knew, no one had ever awakened to find us gone, not even Beth, still breathing deeply in sleep when I quietly crept back into bed, taking care to brush the dirt off my feet. Had anyone destined to follow us on our nighttime excursions, they'd have seen nothing more outrageous than two children skipping in the moonlight, laughing under the stars. Luke and I found our mountain endlessly fascinating by day. By night, it was magical.

I could tell Marissa was angry with her mother as soon as I'd answered her knock, but while I didn't know the reasons Beth had chosen to go to the diner so early in the morning, I didn't think she'd meant it as a slight to Marissa. "I'll get cleaned up and dressed while you get to know your grandmother," I'd told her, "then as soon as I touch base with Evan, we'll go find your mom."

Forty-five minutes later, leaving my mother to the care of her Home Health nurse and stepping onto the street, Kay had met us at the door to the diner, coffee in hand. "Y'all don't look quite as rough as Beth did," she'd said, "but I imagine this might still come in handy." As we reached gratefully for the paper cups, I wondered briefly if Marissa was allowed to drink coffee. Before I could ask, she'd closed her eyes, held the cup to her nose, and inhaled deeply. "Yum," she'd said, "this is even better than Starbucks."

Standing in the doorway, Kay had chuckled. "I figured you for a Starbucks girl." Turning to me, she'd said, "All the teens drink it, you know."

How Kay could have known that was beyond me, but I took her at her word. "Beth left about twenty minutes ago," she said, answering my question before it could be asked. "I reckon you know where she's gone to."

I did, indeed. Thanking Kay, I'd turned to Marissa and asked, "Are you ready for a hike?" She had looked thrilled at the proposition. "I was hoping that was on the agenda for to-day," she'd said gesturing towards her feet, which I saw were clad in soft hiking boots. "I came prepared."

Moments later, as we stepped from the road and moved towards the burbling sound of Rugged Creek, I saw that the path we'd made as children was no longer visible, but the bank just beside the creek was still relatively free from the thick brush and vines that crowded the base of the mountain, no doubt kept clear by the elderly men from town who had always loved to gather on early weekend mornings, the sun not yet visible in the sky, to fish for trout. Luke and I had been known to spy on the ragtag crew from time to time, I told Marissa, hiding in the bushes sometimes, or sometimes—less often— peeking out of a natural cave that had formed at some point in the distant past from boulders no longer able to resist the call of gravity.

If the old men took the art of fishing seriously, they took the art of gossip no less so. As a child, I had assumed men to be the primary proponents of gossip. It was only after I was grown that I learned this was a description generally reserved for women, and I found it difficult to believe. After all, my mother didn't socialize. She never joined quilting bees or gardening clubs, and Sundays were more likely to find the adults of our family nursing throbbing heads and upset stomachs rather than polishing Sunday shoes and reviewing the Bible for marked passages. I had no occasion to observe the women of town during their social gatherings in order to witness what they did or did not do. But the men! Those under the erroneous assumption that women love nothing more than to indulge in the occasional salacious chinwag at the expense of friends and neighbors have obviously never spied on a group of old men fishing.

I can still see them clearly, five or six men, rarely less, sometimes more, mostly retired, seated on rocks, fallen logs, and upturned buckets. To a man, they wore jeans or stained khaki work pants paired with plaid cotton shirts unbuttoned to reveal bellies gone soft and rounded with age. A spattering of gray hairs resided across broad chests once strong from decades of manual labor, now sagging tiredly, relaxed somehow, content in flaccidity. John Deere, Redman Tobacco, and Thundering Herd were popular cap choices, some pushed back to reveal lined foreheads decidedly whiter than the faces they overhung, others pulled so low eyes were barely visible under the broad brims, and ears stuck out at nearly ninety-degree angles.

They hacked and spat and stuffed pinches of snuff between lip and gum, all the while talking, talking, talking, as if making up for years spent in the vacuum of dark, damp mines, or listening to the endless clack of steel along parallel tracks, or time rendered mute by the grind and growl of earth-moving machinery. They argued, too, about politics (*damned socialist!*), the United Mine Workers of America (*bastards*, said one; *heroes*, said another), the ability of the Sons of Marshall to rebuild (*crying shame*, was the general consensus).

They also argued over who the real winner of the Great Fish-Off of '63 was (Eugene Cooper had the popular vote, while Jimmy Williamson took home the prize due to a technicality involving lack of clarity—future participants were apprised that one species of trout did indeed *not* substitute for another), which pie of Peggy's was the best (key lime, without a doubt), and who—dare I even say it—had the best 'shine in the county. As a child, I was proud to overhear my father's name so often mentioned. It may be seen as pathetic, but as an adult, in spite of everything, I remain strangely gratified that my father was at least the best at *something.*

I shared these stories with Marissa as we walked, taking our time. It was a beautiful morning, and although I didn't know exactly what Beth was seeking, I wanted to give her time alone enough to find it without interruption. Meanwhile, I noticed Marissa had taken off her boots as we walked, tying the laces together and slinging them around her neck. She was tentatively inching her way towards the water as we talked. The spring rains and snowmelts were long past, the water no more than a foot or so deep up by the bank, and crystal clear to the bottom. What the hell, I thought, and stopped to take off my own shoes, rolling up my pant legs to join her.

Marissa squealed at the rush of cold water against her shins, making me laugh. I'd forgotten how cold the creek was, and I shivered for a minute, digging my toes into the cool mud, feeling not so much like a forty-two-year-old woman as the young girl I'd been the last time I'd buried my feet into the dark mud of Rugged Creek. Minnows darted around our ankles, disoriented by our sudden intrusion, and water insects skated across the surface, seeking shelter in the shallow water around a stand of cattails. *Cossack asparagus*, I remembered, and pointed the plants out to Marissa. "In the fall," I told her, "we used to come here, Beth, Luke, and I, and dig up the shoots."

"Why?" Marissa asked, reaching out to stroke the furry brown flower.

"They're edible," I told her, and laughed at the expression on her face. "They taste sort of like cucumbers. We'd dig the shoots up, wash them in the creek, and sit down and eat them fresh." I sensed her question before she asked it. "Before we leave," I promised, "we'll dig up a shoot." I was rewarded with a smile that lit up her whole face.

I wasn't sure what Beth would think of my promise, but I knew if her reaction the previous night was any indication, she wouldn't appreciate my sharing of stories with Marissa. I'd been a practicing aunt for less than twenty-four hours and already I was breaking rules and overstepping bounds, but Marissa made for such an attentive audience I was unwilling to sidestep her questions. I wouldn't be so disrespectful as to share Beth's stories with her, but I would share my own.

The mention of a cave had piqued Marissa's interest. "You said you and ... Uncle Luke ..." She hesitated, seemingly unsure what to call the uncle she'd never had opportunity to meet. "You said you guys had hidden in a cave. What sort of cave?" She produced a hairband from her front pocket and captured her hair into a loose knot on top of her head as we moved forward, the current rippling around our knees. The unconscious movement reminded me of Beth, whose long hair had been a source of annoyance for her; she'd rarely left it down. "Do you think it's still there?"

Luke and I had discovered the little cave on one of the many late afternoons we used to escape the discomfort of our shack by the creek. Chores finished and homework completed, I don't know that we ever defined precisely what it was we wanted to escape, or if we even acknowledged it; we knew only that we preferred the scent of decaying vegetation and damp earth to that of cigarette smoke and booze, the sound of bird calls and rustling tree tops to that of profanity and drunken laughter. Both of us fans of Wilson Rawls' *Where the Red Fern Grows*, we often spent our free time in search of "the blackberry patches, and the huckleberry hills." Finding "the fishermen" to complete the ruminations of Billy Colman seemed like nothing less than providence.

We had vivid imaginations, Luke and I, and the solitude provided by the nearly impenetrable forest provided us ample opportunity to fantasize all sorts of exploits. We first came across the little cave one chilly evening when, in fear for our lives from the saber-tooth tiger we imagined stalking us through the woods on monstrous clawed feet, we scrambled for a place to hide. I must have been no older than twelve that cool fall evening, and Luke only ten.

By the late seventies, the plight of the middle child had been studied and debated *ad nauseum*, and I suppose given the literature of that time, I should have spent my childhood the very picture of angst and resentment, boxed in as I was by a serious, solemn older sister and a mischievous, charming younger brother. Having no knowledge of what the experts of that time expected of me, what I felt in actuality was lucky. If what I needed was counsel from a feminine perspective, I had my sister. If what I needed was excitement, I had Luke, who no doubt saved us from a terrible end that evening when he spied the narrow opening and pulled me through to join him on the cold, damp floor, out of reach of the tiger we could almost feel breathing at our backs.

The fact that someone had discovered our hideout before us only added to the mystique. A blanket, filthy and torn, lay against the back wall of the cave, and a fire pit of sorts had been arranged just to the right of the opening below which we crouched. A layer of dust and leaves covered both, and it was evident whomever the intruder (for that was how we thought of the person who had dared to inhabit what we already thought of as *our* cave) had not been in residence for a long time.

Outside our safe haven, we determined the saber-tooth had retreated, no doubt spurred to leave by the fact that the sun was quickly setting and we had to be home before dark. We began the long climb home thrilled with our discovery, determined to return as soon as possible to further explore our new hideout. As it turned out, we did return, many times, and though we searched for clues in true *Encyclopedia Brown* fashion, we never did discover the identity of the previous tenant.

As Marissa and I wound our way slowly up the mountain, I found myself thinking about her question, wondering if the cave was still there, and if it was, how many other young explorers had visited it over the decades I'd been gone. Perhaps Marissa and I would have the opportunity to search for it. Perhaps, I thought, Beth and I could even show her the shack in which we'd grown up. But that was for another day. Today, we wouldn't be climbing that far up the mountain. Instead, our destination was the Rugged Creek Bridge. As difficult as it was to revisit the place our Luke had died, I knew that was where I'd find Beth.

Chapter 25

Beth Pritchett Sloan

If I am to be completely honest, I must admit I was never a happy child. Whereas Naomi was known to be sensitive and sweet and Luke was known to be playful and mischievous, I was simply solemn. I did not laugh with the ease of my siblings, nor was I creative enough or imaginative enough to want to participate in the high adventures Luke and Naomi fancied themselves sharing on their escapades into the mountains.

I wasn't a natural storyteller, nor was I particularly amusing, virtually guaranteeing that whatever anger my father felt towards me could not be diffused by charm. Consequently, I was not the sort of person to step in, placing myself front and center, to protect one of my siblings as Luke and Naomi often did. That isn't to say I didn't love my siblings. I did. But my need for self-preservation outranked my need to protect those whose ability to self-protect was stronger than my own.

We all had our burdens, and I felt unable to bear more than had been bequeathed me by the simple action of my birth. I was unwilling to step into a conflict unless forced, preferring to view silently from the shadows in order to glean whatever information I could so as to avoid finding myself in similar circumstances. Perhaps I was a coward, but it seemed to me my siblings were better equipped, having been granted more talents of avoidance and persuasion than I.

I was also angry with my mother, perpetually so, from as early as I can remember. That may seem strange, given it was my father who left strap marks across my back, but my father made no bones about the fact he was a bastard. There was never a doubt about where he stood, or where we stood in relation to him. We were his property; he could do with us as he pleased. There was no presupposition of love; there were no gestures of affection. We knew exactly what he expected of us, and we knew the consequences if we failed to deliver. There was a stark honesty about our relationship with our father that wasn't present with my mother.

My mother was a chameleon, her temperament as inconstant as the wind. It's true she was capable at times of showing affection, but her affection couldn't be trusted. I learned early on to keep my distance, preferring the stability of my own self-imposed separation from her to the instability of her moods.

Luke, too, often stood apart from my mother, but not for the same reasons as I. Whereas my isolation was rooted in fear of rejection, Luke's was rooted in independence. Quite simply, Luke didn't need my mother. Luke was the only one of the three of us who seemed innately content with life as it was. Not only had I never heard him lament the state of our family, as Naomi and I were wont to do, I daresay Luke never even considered how aberrant our circumstances really were. He hunted and fished; he explored known trails and created new ones; he played with cousins and listened rapt with attention when uncles told stories.

Luke was an adventurous child, and if nothing else, our family suited those needs quite well. I wonder, sometimes, what would have become of Luke had he been given the chance to grow up. I wonder if his complacency would have lent itself to a productive life, free from the angst that had dogged me, or if instead he would have settled, taking up his spot beside the cousins and uncles Naomi and I wanted so much to escape. The speculation frightens me.

Unlike Luke and me, Naomi desperately needed recognition from our mother. It was almost as if, ever the optimist, Naomi believed she could win our mother's affection through sheer persistence. Sometimes she was rewarded for her efforts, but other times my mother would snap and snarl, pushing her away, leaving Naomi to stand alone, crestfallen, wondering what she might have done to cause our mother's rejection.

In reality, Naomi didn't have to do anything to earn rejection from my mother. None of us did. My mother's acceptance or rejection of us was determined by my father. He was, in essence, her drug of choice, and she abandoned everything else—everyone else—for him.

That was precisely what I had been trying to explain to Mark during our phone conversation the previous night. "She was addicted to him," I said, "and neglected us in the process." Mark had always wanted to know more about my history. Naturally, Kay's letter and my trip to West Virginia had worked to open lines of communication long rusted shut. I was actually enjoying our talk, but then Mark grew quiet and I heard that quick intake of breath I knew so well, followed by a moment of hesitation, an indication he was about to say something he knew might not be well received. I tensed, already defensive.

"Is that really how you see it?" he asked. "As an addiction?"

"Of course. How else would you define it? What do those pamphlets in your office say? An addiction is the continued use of a mood-altering drug, regardless of the consequences. That explains my mother perfectly. My father was her mood-altering drug. Everything she did, from the way she treated us to the way she lived, or *didn't* live, for that matter, depended on my father's reactions. And we suffered for it. She just wasn't there for us, Mark, not in any real sense, and I don't mean she didn't attend PTA meetings or sew costumes for the school play, although she certainly didn't, I mean she stood by and did nothing—*nothing*, Mark—while that horrible man poured whiskey down our throats and beat us black and blue."

I stopped, breathing hard, alarmed at the magnitude of my anger. I had deliberately buried those memories for years, but in spite of my best intentions, my resentment was frighteningly close to the surface.

"I think you're absolutely right," Mark finally said, and I could tell he was weighing his words carefully. "Without a doubt, she was codependent. And that surely affected all of you in various ways."

I felt my antennae go up. I knew Mark well enough to know he never spoke recklessly, and his medical jargon always put me on edge. "What do you mean?"

"Beth," he said, and I clenched my fists. "Your family history, what little you've told me, is horrendous. Don't you think that has to have affected you?" Clearly, the question was rhetorical, because he didn't wait for an answer. Mark's questions to me were often rhetorical. "I mean," he continued without pause, "you're obviously not like your father, or even your mother. But, sweetheart ..." He stopped, and I tensed even more. Then he began again. "The dysfunction, the alcohol. Honey, I don't know any way to say this other than to just say it. I'm worried about you."

I worked hard to keep myself composed. "Worried about me? Why?" I knew, though. I did. In my most honest, innermost heart, I knew exactly what he was going to say.

"Beth ..." And again that pause that I was beginning to loathe, followed by a deep sigh, which was, in its way, even worse than the silence. "You seem so unhappy. Sometimes I worry that maybe you use your evening cocktail as a way to feel better. After what you've shared with me tonight, it makes even more sense. You're medicating yourself against the painful memories of your past."

He couldn't have been any kinder with his accusations, but I was furious, not only because I had known where he was going with this conversation, but because of the pomposity of his statement. I was his wife, damn him, and I resented—detested, actually—both the audacity of his diagnosis and the feeling I'd always had that I was a specimen to Mark, something to be studied and picked apart. I was the woman who gathered his dirty underwear from the bathroom floor. I would have recognized his snore from two doors down; I could identify the drool pattern on his pillow. Who was he, to diagnose me? And so even though I knew he was right, my anger boiled over.

"Damn you, Mark, you son of a bitch. How dare you?" I asked. Shortly thereafter, I hung up the phone. But his indictments stayed with me, joining those of Luke, and of my children. And of myself.

Sitting on the bridge above Rugged Creek, legs dangling over the side, I gazed into the water trickling past below me. The sun was now fully over the mountains, and the creek sparkled under its light, the reflection broken periodically by the edges of rocks only partially submerged. The waters of Rugged Creek were always low in the heat of summer. The dislodged rocks and boulders that were hidden by snowmelt and spring rains lay exposed along the banks and bed.

The bravest among us had jumped off the bridge as children, in the springtime when the water was high, an action our parents forbade but we engaged in, regardless. We cannonballed into the rushing water, knocked temporarily breathless by the frigid temperature, well aware of the rocks that lurked down in its depths but trusting they were too deep to cause us harm. Luke had loved to jump off the bridge, partly, I think, because it never failed to elicit screams from Naomi and me. Luke was fearless, but not even he, reckless as he was, would have been foolish enough to jump off the bridge when the water was low.

Why? I remember them whispering, the good ladies of the church, the men from town, the children from school, all sweating in their Sunday best as the sun beat down on our heads. *Why would he have done that? Surely he knew the creek was too shallow. Surely he knew how dangerous it would be. What a pity. I knew it was only a matter of time until something like this happened. Poor Geraldine!* They hid their faces behind their fans in the cemetery at Cedar Hollow Baptist Church and they whispered, cutting their eyes towards our mother while Luke's coffin was lowered into the ground.

The memory brought me shame. I was exhausted, mentally and physically wrung out, and as the sun warmed my shoulders some of the anger that had consumed me during the night, indeed for most of my life, slipped away to reveal what I'd tried to avoid all along: sorrow. I was sorry.

Such a simple phrase, one I'd said more often out of habit or social expectation than true penitence, but that morning, as the all too familiar anger drained away, I felt it down to my core. It constricted my chest and lodged in my throat. It stung my eyes and sapped the strength from my body. I was sorry, truly and rightly sorry, and I didn't know how to even begin to correct the wrongs I'd committed. Some things simply cannot be fixed. Grief, long suppressed, rose up with such force it threatened to overwhelm me. I dropped my head into my hands and let it come. If it destroyed me, so be it; I welcomed it. Not only that; I deserved it. Below me, I heard the ceaseless rippling of the creek, and it seemed to call to me. The creek knew.

No, Luke would never have jumped when the waters were low. And, in fact, he hadn't.

I'm sorry, Luke. I'm sorry. I'm sorry. I'm sorry.

Chapter 26

Naomi Pritchett Wells

By the time I was fifteen, my desire—and imagination—for dangerous wilderness adventures with Luke had largely waned. I had discovered boys by then, or more accurately, they had discovered me, and I enjoyed the attention. I had also discovered nail polish, curlers, and lipstick, much more appealing accoutrements to me than mud or leeches. Unlike Beth, I was a social child, and I relied on my friends and their mothers for beauty advice. I took some pride in my appearance once I was *cleaned up*, as they used to say.

Luke was disappointed at the change in me; I remember that. "You've turned into a sissy," he told me once, as he slouched against the doorframe of the room I shared with Beth. He was dressed in his typical summer attire: shirtless and barefoot, his hands shoved loosely into the pockets of those ever-present cutoff shorts, the fringe of denim threads unraveled and hanging below his knees.

"In case you haven't noticed," I responded, glancing dismissively at his reflection in the cloudy dressing table mirror as I snapped closed one of the dozens of pink plastic curlers I had affixed to my head, "I'm a *girl*."

Beth had brought those curlers home, a gift from Kay Langley at the diner where Beth had begun working. "I don't have enough hair for them," she had reportedly told Beth. "And Lord knows Emily has enough curlers to style the hair of every woman in Cedar Hollow. Maybe you can find a use for them." I don't recall Beth ever using them, but *I* certainly had. They were an unaccustomed luxury, and the discomfort of sleeping in the contraptions had been well worth the effort.

Just the previous week I'd attracted the attention of not one, but *two* of the Cooper family boys.

From his position against the doorframe Luke snorted. "You look more like an alien than a girl, with those stupid things all over your head. Come on, Naomi. It's almost dark. You can go gigging with those things on. Ain't nobody there to see you but the frogs."

I didn't budge, not that time or many others that final summer, and I have often felt guilty since his death, remembering how frequently I turned him down when he tried to tempt me into accompanying him on his jaunts. What would it have cost me, I wonder now, to have gone with him on one last excursion through the forest, dodging imaginary lawmen and bandits and Sasquatch, gigging frogs or baiting hooks—or in my case, chasing frogs out of his path and unbaiting hooks, much to Luke's annoyance.

It was a wonder he wanted me along, as much grief as I gave him. But he did, and I'm sorry now that in my fifteenth year I suddenly found myself with no time for the silly childhood games we'd always played, and no interest in the muck and slime of Rugged Creek.

I have often marveled, since then, at our compulsion to see the future exactly as the present is. We assume that what has been will always be. What mother, knowing a child's visit to her lap is his last, wouldn't hold onto that child for an instant longer? What sister, knowing the vision of her strong, tanned brother in cutoff denim shorts would soon be replaced by that of a coffin, wouldn't throw the curlers aside and join him on a warm summer night?

But we always miss the crucial moments. We videotape birthdays and weddings, post pictures of holidays and family reunions, but how many of us recognize the final moment—not just of life, but of the makings of life—when it comes? It was for this reason, I realized as I waded alongside Marissa through the clear waters of Rugged Creek, that I had never had children. All those unknown last moments overwhelmed me. I couldn't bear the multitude of losses. The last midnight feeding, the last nursery rhyme, the last game of pat-a-cake.

The last kiss to heal a hurt, the last holding of hands crossing the street, the last band recital. I simply couldn't bear it. I don't know, in retrospect, if my fear of loss came from our loss of Luke, or of my loss of any sense of home. I couldn't imagine surviving the loss of a child. It was that most recent realization, that we—I—brought such pain to our mother, that chipped away the walls I had resurrected so many years ago, and left me raw. Or perhaps more honestly, it was the realization that I lost out too, on whatever it was my mother had to give me.

I realized in a flash of insight that was also the reason I wrote fantasy. Anything else was too close to home. Being chased by werewolves and vampires was infinitely easier than being chased by the ghosts of family. I abandoned one, and made a living from the other. I was not immune to the irony, though it had only recently been forced to my attention: That which I sought to escape had, in fact, defined me.

I had also given up jumping from the bridge that long ago summer, seeing as if with adult eyes the potential hazards of such a jump, even with the water at its highest. But Luke, I knew, continued to enjoy his madcap stunts, no more noticing the jagged rocks along the creek bed than he noticed the dangers of the stills behind our Rugged Creek shack. Luke was an adventurer, an explorer. I suppose in hindsight his death shouldn't have been unexpected, given the dares he so often obliged, but it was, nevertheless. I don't know what possessed him to jump during the heat of summer, with the water notoriously low, but I did know he would never have intentionally hurt himself.

I saw Beth before she saw us, sitting on the bridge, legs dangling, framed by the sun at her back. For a moment, time stood still. How many times, I wondered, had I seen my sister sitting in just that pose, atop Rugged Creek Bridge? It had been one of her favorite spots. It had been a favorite spot for all the Pritchett children, cousins and siblings alike. I wondered if she had found what she was looking for.

I did not call Marissa's attention to her mother. I'm not sure why I didn't. Maybe I wanted to witness Marissa's enjoyment of the day for a minute longer, or maybe some part of me wanted to protect Beth. I don't know what made me think she needed protecting, but that was the distinct feeling I got, looking up at her as she perched on the side of the bridge, her hands on the wooden rail, legs swinging in the wind. I shivered, in spite of the sun at my face.

Although Beth was the eldest, in some ways I'd always felt protective towards her. Luke and I had always had each other, but Beth was often alone. She rarely accompanied us on our expeditions. No doubt she felt too old to engage in our juvenile pursuits. Age differences aside, Beth could seem so distant and sad that I worried about her at times. In spite of the years, that instinct didn't seem to have waned, particularly given the scenario—and Marissa's reaction to it—with the bottle of wine the previous night.

More than once as a girl sharing the stale, sweaty sheets with Beth, I'd fallen asleep with the unmistakable scent of corn liquor wafting gently across my face as she slept soundly beside me. I was too naïve to think much of it back then. After all, that smell permeated my childhood. Inhaling it as I drifted into sleep was not strange to me. Nor had I thought of it since. My childhood was a world unto itself, different and separate from the life I had made. It was only since Beth's overly giddy presentation of the wine the previous night, coupled with Marissa's obvious discomfort, that the memory had resurfaced. As an adult, the ramifications were troubling, to say the least.

As I reflected on my initial impression of Beth the previous day, coupled with Marissa's reaction to her mother's supposed excitement at remembering the bottle of wine, I suddenly saw the devastating effects of our childhood in a way I hadn't before. I don't know how I managed to escape the alcohol in our genes. Perhaps I should have thanked my mother. After all, I never witnessed her sampling the batch, not once. To the best of my recollection, my mother kept to herself; rarely did I see her interacting with my father's relatives, scattered throughout our lives though they were. She moved silently among them, present but apart.

"There's my mom." Marissa pointed towards the bridge, drawing me from my memories. "She looks like a kid, up there like that," she said, shading her eyes from the sun, a note of pleasure in her voice. She moved toward the bank, but I stopped her.

"Let me go to her first, Marissa." I wanted to explain the unease I felt, but I couldn't put it into words. There were things Marissa didn't know, dark shadows of our past. I knew Beth was struggling with those demons, and again I felt the need not only to protect Beth, but also to protect Marissa.

To my surprise, she didn't argue. Instead, she turned to look at me for a long moment, then shrugged her agreement. She bent to dip her hands in the cold water of the creek, splashing the water over her face. "Okay," she said, wiping her arm across her mouth. "Let me know when I can come."

I nodded, and she smiled such a sweet smile it tugged at my heart. "It'll be okay," I told her, reaching out to touch her cheek, not simply to comfort her, but because I believed it to be true. It *would* be okay, not only what was happening on the bridge of Rugged Creek, but whatever was happening between Marissa and Beth back in Tennessee.

Leaving Marissa to the creek, I began the long, tangled climb to the bridge. Evan and I both belonged to the local gym, but no matter how refined a gym is, no matter how well equipped, it simply cannot compare with a hike up a West Virginia mountainside on a humid summer morning. I was winded and sweaty by the time I reached the bridge, and I took a moment to catch my breath before stepping forward to go to Beth.

She didn't look at me, didn't move at all, until I settled myself beside her, my breathing back to normal, hanging my legs off the bridge and gripping the railing next to her. The breeze was cool against my face, and I found comfort in that. It was unbelievable to me that the bridge had seemed so manageable to me as a child. The creek looked full of dangers as I gazed upon Marissa below.

I looked at Beth, and she turned to face me.

"Do you feel him here?" I asked, because I knew that was what we were both searching for.

She smiled at me, and the smile made her look youthful. Tired, but peaceful. "He's not here," she said. "He's gone now. Luke is gone, but he forgave me before he left."

The serenity of Beth's expression brought me hope. "Now what?" I asked.

"We need to go to Mother," she said, and reached to squeeze my hand. "I need to tell you what happened. It's been too long." She looked down at Marissa, who was bent over examining something along the bank of the creek. "She's barefoot," she said. "In the mud. Who would have thought?" She shook her head, incredulous, then turned to me again. "How is she? Mother, I mean."

I had to think before answering. "The word I want to use is *different*," I said, "but I don't know if that's accurate, because I don't really know what she was like before. Do you know, until now I don't remember ever having a real conversation with our mother?"

Beth nodded. "We didn't," she agreed. "We answered questions and followed orders. We didn't talk, not even on the good days, because we never knew how long it would last. Is she angry?"

I shook my head. "No. I think she probably was for a long time, but I don't think she is now. She's too ..." I searched again for the right words. "Too worn down, I think, to be angry."

"Worn down," Beth repeated. "That's a feeling I can understand."

We sat in silence for a time before I took her hand, and we stood.

Chapter 27

Geraldine Porter Pritchett

I let Betsy go this morning. I hated to do it, in a way. She's a right nice girl, but I reckon I can take care of myself, now I've a mind to. After Luke died, I took to my bed wanting to go with him, until I realized I had to get up to take care of my girls. Even after I saw they was gone, I stayed up waiting for them. I waited a long, long time.

Then Junior died, and I got it set in my mind the girls wasn't never coming back, so I decided to finally lay down for good. But they came, after all, and here I am getting up again. I am beginning to see it just ain't meant for me to lay down and die.

I napped for a couple of hours after Naomi and Marissa went off looking for Beth. I didn't think I'd be able to, but the body can only take so much, and I ain't in the best of health. To my relief, I woke up feeling right fresh. Betsy helped me bathe and dress real quick, though I told her she didn't need to, and I spent the last few minutes sitting by the window, watching for the girls to come back. I was not afraid this time. I knew they'd come, even Beth, and sure enough there they are, walking side by side down the road, with Marissa in the middle.

I take some time to look at them, most especially Beth. My eyesight is too far gone for me to see much more than shapes, but I know Beth's walk. Naomi was always quick in her step, like her daddy, and Marissa takes after them in that way. But Beth was slow. I always got the feeling, watching Beth walk up the path on her way back from wherever she'd been, that it took all her strength to make her feet bring her back home. That looks to still be true.

I hear them on the stairs, talking to Erma, before they knock at my door. I holler at them to come on in, and Erma comes first, carrying a tray of muffins and honeydew. Right behind her is Marissa, her cheeks flushed pink from the morning air. She's taken to our mountains, I can see that. She moves to sit on the floor next to me and there's Naomi, thanking Erma and clearing off a spot on the table so Erma can set down the tray. And finally, at the back of the group, standing still in my doorway and looking at me, is Beth.

I don't raise up to go to her, though I have to grip the arms of my chair to hold myself still, because I know that ain't what she'd want me to do. Even as a little girl, Beth was standoffish with me. She kept her distance, and after a while I gave her the space she wanted. It hurt me to do it; there's times a woman wants to reach out to her child. But Beth didn't want me, and I would not force her to have me. I will not force her now, either.

Beth waits on Erma to leave and Naomi to settle herself before she pulls a chair across from the three of us and sits. Her face is tired, and she looks older than I had expected. I know she ain't a young woman anymore, but for some reason I am surprised at Beth's appearance in a way I wasn't at Naomi's. She looks unwell. I want to ask if she's all right, but I don't. I wait, because there ain't much else I can do.

Finally, she sits forward, rubbing her hands along her thighs like she's drying off her palms. "There are things I need to tell you," she says, "and I need you to hear everything before you interrupt." She looks from one of us to the other, and we all nod. I don't know when Naomi and Marissa reached to take my hands, but I find that we are holding tight to each other.

"I killed Luke," she says, and the room spins in front of my eyes. I feel Naomi's arm around me, holding me up, and I hear Marissa's sharp cry beside me.

"But so did you, in a way," my eldest daughter says to me.

Chapter 28

Beth Pritchett Sloan

I saw my mother swoon before me, and I must admit it brought me some sense of satisfaction. I had spent my entire adult life buried under an insurmountable burden of guilt. It was true, what I had told them. I *had* killed Luke. I hadn't meant to, and God knows I'd give my own life in place of his if that were possible. Regardless, it was me in the end who was directly responsible for his death. But I also meant the second part of what I'd said. It was my mother, too, and my father, who killed Luke. They weren't there when he died, as I was, but they set in motion a chain of events that killed him just as surely as I had.

My goal that day, baring my soul to the three women across from me, was to heal myself and my family. Not the family I'd been born into, but the family I'd created. I could only do that by getting everything out into the open. If I could heal my family of origin in the process, I wanted to do that, too, but it wasn't my top priority, and I wasn't at all sure it was even possible. Some of the things I had to say would undoubtedly cause pain. I waited until the women across from me settled again and continued.

"Naomi," I asked, "do you remember what Daddy gave each of us on our thirteenth birthday? It shouldn't be hard to remember since it's the only gift he ever gave us." That was true; my father had only given us one gift, if it could be called that, and even then his motivations were more about him than they were about us.

Naomi sat forward in the chair, her hand clasped with both Marissa's and my mother's, their intertwined fingers resting on my mother's knees. "I do," she said. "A pint. Or what was left of one, anyway. He released us from taster duty and gave us a pint."

Indeed he had. Pritchetts required customers to provide their own quart-sized Mason jars when ordering 'shine, but for personal consumption they preferred a flask-shaped pint bottle with a cork stopper, no doubt because it fit better in the back pockets of the men as they went about their work. At any rate, shortly after dinner on my thirteenth birthday, our father had motioned for me to follow him outside.

I was terrified, my brain performing mental calisthenics in a desperate attempt to remember what I might have done wrong. The day had been a quiet one, cold and crisp. I'd come directly home from school and completed my chores before settling at the table to do homework, a book report, I remembered, on Robert Cormier's *The Chocolate Wars*. I was not a big reader, but I had enjoyed the book, so the assignment had been easy for me. I was finished in plenty of time to help my mother in the kitchen.

Dinner was uneventful, and I had nearly forgotten it was my birthday when my mother surprised me by setting a pineapple upside-down cake in the center of the table. My mother was kind to us in that way. She never failed to bake our favorite cake on our birthdays. I was even more astounded when she handed me a small box wrapped in the Sunday comics. Everyone watched as I opened it and gently peeled back the tissue paper to reveal a spoon ring nestled underneath. I looked at my mother, astonished.

"Billy May told me you'd been down to the store, lookin' at it," she said, and I sent a silent thank you to Billy May Platte, the owner of Mr. Smith's General Store. "Now, it ain't new," Momma said, leaning over my shoulder to see it as I slipped it on my finger. "Billy May said Sue Ann Hayden gave it to her and told her to sell it for whatever she thought was a right price, and you know Billy May. She worked with me on it. Said Sue Ann found it when she was cleanin' out a box in the attic. I reckon it was something left over from her last husband, the one who run off and left her, and she just wanted to get it out of her sight."

Billy May was right. I had been in the store admiring the ring, but I would never have asked for it. We didn't ask for things back then. I was grateful to Billy May, and even more grateful to my mother. I finally managed to gather my wits about me enough to tell her so. She patted me on the shoulder and smiled a rare smile. "Thirteen is a special age," she said. "You're becomin' a young woman now."

I was still basking in the glow of the unexpected gift when my father motioned me to the door. Maybe, I had thought, he was angry that my mother had spent the money. Or maybe I'd been so dumbfounded I hadn't adequately expressed my appreciation. I didn't know the reason he wanted me outside, but I knew from past history it couldn't be good. Naomi and Luke both shot me a look as I rose to follow him, and I could tell they were as concerned as I was. I shrugged at them, a silent communication. *What did I do?* They shrugged back, as puzzled as I, before I followed my father out into the dark night.

It was windy, I remember, the gusts slicing through the loose cotton weave of my sweater as if I wore nothing at all. I hadn't taken time to grab my coat; it would not have been wise to keep my father waiting. I also knew better than to question my father, so I walked behind him in silence, my heart pounding with fear. We circled around behind the house and started down the nearly hidden path that led to the stills. We hadn't gone far before we came to one of the many clearings in which my relatives loved to gather. True to form, there they were, an assortment of uncles and in-laws, all male, huddled around a small fire to keep warm. They grew quiet as we approached, and Uncle Bobby, one of the older of the ten Pritchett siblings, moved aside and motioned for me to sit next to him.

I was not afraid of my uncles, exactly, but I was cautious. While they had never hurt me or my siblings physically, they were known to be as coldhearted as their father, and my father in turn. So I sat as directed, but I remained alert, ready to run if needed, though I most certainly knew I couldn't escape. My father stood across the fire from me, unspeaking.

Next to me, Uncle Bobby produced a pint bottle from somewhere and tilted his head back, taking a small sip. He passed it to Uncle Wayne on his other side, and so it continued around the circle until, finally, it was handed to me. I held the bottle, now half gone, towards Uncle Bobby, but he shook his head and pointed at my father, who finally spoke.

"You're the oldest Pritchett of your generation, so the tradition gets handed down to you just like our daddy handed it down to us," he said. "You're nearly grown now, too old for taster duty. Take the bottle. It's yours as a rite of passage. Do what you want with it. It don't make no difference to me."

I didn't know how to respond, but it hardly mattered. As soon as my father had finished what he had to say, conversation started up again around the campfire. No one expected me to speak; my role in that particular family drama was over. I waited long enough to ensure I wouldn't be noticed—or that if I were, it wouldn't matter—before I crept back down the dark path toward home.

I was surprised to see Naomi and Luke waiting for me on the porch, shivering in the darkness. Naomi held my coat out to me and I accepted it gratefully. "What happened?" she asked. "Did you get a whipping?"

I shook my head. "No, I didn't get a whipping. I got a pint." I held the bottle up to the light spilling out of the unadorned living room window.

"A *pint*?" she asked as Luke took the bottle from my hand and sniffed at the cork. "Why?"

"Apparently it's a rite of passage. Something the Pritchetts do when their kids turn thirteen," I hastened to add, cutting Luke off before he could ask what a rite of passage was. I laughed through the chattering of my teeth. "So when we turn thirteen we can either go down to the church and get baptized," I said, "or we can just stay up here and drink whiskey."

Luke replaced the cork and handed the bottle back to me. "What are you going to do with it?"

"I don't know," I answered him. "Daddy said he didn't care what I did with it."

"I'd throw it away," said Naomi, her breath steaming in the cold night air. "If I ever get to stop doing taster duty, I don't ever want to taste it again."

Poor Naomi had suffered through more than her fair share of it by that time. Truthfully, by the time Luke had reached school age there were so many younger cousins underfoot it was rare for either Luke or me to be summoned. I had learned to submit, and Luke had never seemed particularly bothered by the experience, but Naomi's distaste remained so apparent it made for an amusing experience for those in attendance; hence, she was beckoned with some regularity.

I suppose it comes as no surprise that I didn't throw it away. No, I waited until Naomi was asleep, then I snuck down to the creek where I sat on the bank with a quilt wrapped around me and got well and truly drunk for the very first time. One thing I'll say for Pritchett liquor: That *pure 'shine* recipe my father was so proud of was stout. I awakened, or more accurately, I came to, sometime before the sun rose, frozen stiff, my hands and feet gone numb from the cold. I crawled to the edge of the bank and vomited, undigested pineapple bits making a splash as they hit the water.

Somehow, I made it back to the house, though I have no memory of it. The next morning I pleaded sickness, which was true, and my mother allowed me to stay home from school. I didn't know if she knew the truth back then, and even with the telling of the story, with my mother and Marissa and Naomi sitting silently before me, I was unable to gauge the depth of her knowledge. She sat perfectly still, her head bowed. I could not see her eyes.

My father, though, he knew. I awakened at some point during the day to see him standing in my doorway. I was too dizzy and nauseous to focus well, but the memory of his smile still repulses me.

Naomi remained true to her word. Two years later, better prepared than I had been, she followed our father to the clearing without fear. She watched the men pass the bottle from hand to hand, mouth to mouth, and accepted it without comment. Like me, she returned to find her siblings waiting for her on the porch, but unlike me, she brought back an empty bottle.

"They gave you an empty bottle?" Luke asked, and Naomi shook her head.

"I poured it out on the trail as soon as I was too far away for them to see. I told you, I never want to taste that stuff again as long as I live."

By that time, I was proficient at sneaking the brew from my father and his brothers, an ounce or two here and there from a discarded bottle either left around the campfire or propped on the cluttered end table beside our sagging couch. The squeezings they'd forced us to endure as children were enough to burn our mouths, but not enough to bring about the buzz I'd found the night of my thirteenth birthday. I never drank to the point of outright drunkenness, not after that first time. I had not enjoyed the resultant hangover, but I had enjoyed the spreading warmth, the immediate buoyancy I felt after a few stolen swallows.

Those times were, quite literally, the only periods during my childhood I felt hopeful. I know now, of course, that it was only the false promise made by liquor, but as a child, I had believed the lie. What a sad summation of my childhood that is.

I was annoyed with Naomi for having dumped hers out. Until that point, some part of me had hoped we could share my secret together. I did not reveal my thoughts to her, however. At least, not until that moment at the Vines and Roses Boarding Home.

Unlike my mother, Naomi and Marissa kept their eyes glued to mine as I spoke. I think Marissa was dumbfounded not so much at the content of what I was saying as by the fact that I was saying it at all. She had grown up with me squarely entrenched in my denial, and for the whole of her life she had begged to know more of my family.

She sat as still as a statue, afraid, maybe, that if she caught my attention by moving, I'd be reminded to send her out of the room. *If you want to stay up late, you should be invisible* we used to tell the children when they were young, when we didn't mind bending the rules a little so long as they didn't inconvenience us with squabbling or tattling. Marissa obviously still remembered that advice.

I don't think Naomi was stunned by any of my revelations. I imagine some part of her had known, even as a child, that I'd nipped into a bottle or two from time to time. She might not have understood the significance of it back then but she surely did as an adult. The dysfunction of our family was not news to Naomi.

Neither, I suspected, was the subsequent mess I'd made of my life. Naomi had always been quick; it wouldn't have taken her long to figure out my family and I were struggling. Her expression as I spoke was a mixture of resignation and regret.

"Do you remember what Luke said when you told us you never wanted to taste corn liquor again as long as you lived?" I asked her.

"He said—" She stopped and cleared her throat. "He said he liked the taste. He said on his thirteenth birthday he planned to stay with the other Pritchett men and finish off the bottle. Of course ..." She closed her eyes briefly. "He was only eleven. He couldn't have known what he was saying."

"Couldn't he have?" I asked, but Naomi didn't answer. "Luke was a Pritchett, too, you know." I pressed her. "He wanted to be accepted not only by our father, but by all the Pritchett men. Maybe he knew exactly what he was saying."

"Enough!"

I was momentarily startled into silence by my mother's furious voice. She raised her head and made eye contact then, and those were the eyes I remembered from my childhood: piercing and angry. "That's enough," she said again. "No more, Beth. I don't want to hear any more."

I met her gaze and held it. Her temper no longer had power over me. "That was always the problem," I said quietly. "But you're going to listen now. You're going to hear everything I have to say."

Chapter 29

Beth Pritchett Sloan

I continued to hold my mother's stare. I would not be intimidated; she would not stop me from speaking the truth about how our lives had been. I wasn't trying to hurt her, but the only way I knew to heal my family was to state the truth, and I was determined to do it. The Pritchett family history was full of lies and deceit. I was tied to that legacy against my will, but I was no longer disposed to sit in silence while it destroyed my life and I in turn destroyed the lives of those I held most dear.

My father was the outward face of our family's dysfunction, but my mother provided the foundation. I had not wanted to return to Cedar Hollow, but once there, I refused to leave without exorcising the demons my family had wrought. Otherwise, what was the purpose? I had to answer only to Marissa on my trip home, and I intended to do that with the clear eyes of sobriety and honesty. *You need to make peace*, Kay's letter had said, but peace was not the answer. Verity was.

After what seemed an eternity, my mother dropped her gaze back to the floor. Naomi and Marissa looked back and forth between the two of us, waiting to see what would happen next. I would not retreat, if that was what they were expecting, and I think both of them, for their own reasons, were glad to realize that.

"As I was saying," I continued, "I think Luke did know what he meant. He talked about it again that last summer, remember, Naomi?"

"I remember," she said. "He was excited about his birthday, and he questioned the two of us nonstop about the meeting by the campfire. He was looking forward to it, I think mainly because he wanted to be included by the men in the family."

I nodded. "That's what I think, too. I think it was more about being a part of the 'Pritchett boys' than it was about drinking moonshine."

There had always been something about the Pritchett identity that called to Luke, maybe because in many ways he *was* a Pritchett. I don't mean Luke was cruel—there wasn't a mean bone in his body—but so many aspects of Luke's personality exemplified the best of what it meant to be a Pritchett. He was strong and fearless, a risk taker and a daredevil. He was unstructured and impulsive, imaginative and creative, happiest when unbound by the chains of convention. Luke was what the Pritchett men *could* have been at their finest.

Luke was also coming of age in the truest sense, on the verge of becoming a young man. He wanted and needed a father figure, and the Pritchett men were all he had. The sad truth of it was, if Luke wanted to be accepted by the men of our family, there was no better way to do it than to sit around the campfire drinking whiskey.

On the evening of his birthday, after we'd shared the Mississippi mud cake and Luke had admired his knife, our father beckoned to him as we had known he would. "Don't wait for me," Luke whispered across the table as he stood, his eyes shining with excitement. "I'm staying with the men tonight." He had sauntered out the door in our father's footsteps, barefoot and bare chested as always, pausing only to flash an impish grin over his shoulder.

As she had done first with me, and then with Naomi, our mother continued cleaning the kitchen as if nothing had happened, handing Naomi a broom and instructing me to take more care with the Depression glass platter she'd inherited from her mother. Naomi and I did as she instructed, all the while trading questioning looks behind her back. How could she not know where my father was taking him?

"I knew where he was goin'."

I stopped, once again interrupted by my mother's voice. This time the words weren't angry, but resigned. I had to lean forward to hear her, looking at Naomi for confirmation. *Did she just say she knew?* The strained expression on Naomi's face validated what I thought I'd heard.

That topic had been the subject of endless discussions between Naomi and me on sleepless nights. We didn't understand how our mother could possibly be oblivious to what we had come to think of as the pint ceremony, but if she knew about it, why would she let it continue? Was she really so ensnared in the Pritchett lifestyle that she somehow lost sight of the fact that giving a thirteen-year-old child a pint of whiskey wasn't a *good* thing? My mother had answered the first question, which only served to emphasize the second.

She let go of Naomi and Marissa and covered her eyes with her hands, as if hiding from her confession. "I didn't know the first time, when he took you, Beth. But I figured out right quick the next mornin' what was wrong with you. Seein' somebody sick with liquor was near about an everyday thing around our place back then, but I hadn't expected it from you. At first I thought you had snuck into it on your own, and I was ready to tan your hide for it, but then your daddy told me what had happened." She lowered her hands and looked at me, her face troubled.

"We fought about it. Oh, we had some jim-dandy fights, your daddy and me. Remember that time I was laid up with flu? I didn't have no flu. My ribs was cracked. And when I left to go visit my aunt in Kentucky? There wasn't no aunt in Kentucky. Porters is known for havin' trouble bearin' babies. My daddy was an only child. I was in the hospital over at Huntington. I see you didn't expect that," she said, as she caught the look I traded with Naomi.

"Y'all thought I just sat down and let him do whatever he pleased with you, but that ain't the truth. I know it could be bad, I know it *was* sometimes, but did you ever once think how much worse it might have been? No, of course you didn't.

I never talked back to him in front of you," she said, "because I never wanted you to see the consequence of it."

She paused, but I think Naomi and I were both too caught off guard to react. She was right. I hadn't thought how much worse it might have been, because I'd had no inkling she'd ever attempted to shield us from our father. I had known firsthand the brutality of the man. I knew his penchant for the strap, and I knew it took little provocation for him to use it. But I had not known my mother shared our suffering at the hands of our father. She had hidden it well. Her revelation didn't excuse the things she'd allowed to happen to us, but it did add an unexpected element, food for thought, at least.

Sitting beside her, a profusion of emotions washed across Naomi's face, and I knew what she must be thinking. Before either of us could ask, my mother spoke again.

"I told him not to take you, Naomi. I tried to make him promise me he wouldn't do that to you and Luke. But he wouldn't listen to me. 'Woman,' he said to me, like he did when he was mad, 'this is what my family has always done and what it will always do, and you ain't goin' to come between us. Mind your place,' he said. 'This ain't none of your concern.'"

"So you let him take me," said Naomi.

"I couldn't stop him," my mother said, and there was an undercurrent of anger to the words. "What would have been worse, Naomi, lettin' him take you there, knowin' he wasn't goin' to hurt you—not really—or lettin' you see him beat the livin' daylights out of me on our kitchen floor?"

I found myself at a loss for words, but Naomi managed to speak for both of us. "So you let him take me," she repeated, "because you knew he wouldn't hurt me." I don't know if our mother picked up on the disbelief so apparent to me in Naomi's voice. Of course it *had* hurt Naomi; it had hurt all of us, culminating in the death of Luke and the destruction of our family.

"He wasn't goin' to whup you that night," our mother said. "Not so long as you went with him. But who's to say what he might have done to any of us if I'd tried to stop him?"

"Why did you stay?" Until then, Marissa had remained quiet, transfixed by our conversation and offering silent comfort to both Naomi and her grandmother.

My mother's face softened at her question. "Child," she said, "where would I have gone? There weren't no shelters for women in Cedar Hollow, and even if there had been, he'd have just come and got me. Where could I have gone, a woman with three children? And I loved him; I did, in spite of it all. I know that don't make no sense, but Junior set me free. My parents meant well; they cared for me, but it wasn't a fit life for a child, shut up in the house that way. I was achin' to get out, and Junior got me out."

Marissa reached out to hug her. I still had my issues with my mother; I wasn't expecting them to soften anytime soon, yet I was proud of Marissa, regardless. I didn't know where she'd learned such compassion, but I suspected it hadn't been from me. No doubt I should have followed her example, but for the moment the years of resentment I'd stoked overrode any compassion I may have felt.

"Did they beat you?" I asked, and my mother turned to me, confused. I asked the question partly in earnest. I'd never heard my mother speak of having been abused by her parents, and I was curious. I also asked because it afforded me the opportunity to place a well-aimed dagger, and I was not above exploiting it. "You said your parents meant well, but it wasn't a fit life for a child. What I want to know is, did they beat you? Dribble whiskey down your throat? Leave you to raise yourself?"

"Beth," Naomi began, but I waved her aside.

"No," my mother answered quietly. "It wasn't like that. They never laid a hand on me, but they squeezed the life out of me just the same."

I peered at my mother, fascinated, I suppose, by her inability to see beyond her own childhood victimization, if it could even be called that. Given the choice between being raised with too much love or not enough, I felt fairly certain I'd choose the former. So her childhood hadn't been picture perfect. That justification for the poor parenting of which she was guilty didn't hold water with me. *For the sins of your fathers you, though guiltless, must suffer,* the Latin poet Horace had written, and I knew firsthand the same was true for mothers and daughters. My mother's inability to look past the resentments she held against her own parents had shaped our childhood in terrible ways.

"I find it interesting that you see your parents' faults so clearly," I said, "but you're so completely blind to your own. Daddy's abuse was only part of the problem. You weren't there for us, in any sense of the word. Do you really not see that?"

Across from me, my mother sat perfectly still, aside from a slight twitching in the muscle of her jaw. The silence in the room was absolute; I could hear a fly buzzing against the outside of the window glass, bumping against it in frustration. My bitterness was so deeply rooted I was prepared to wait forever, if that's how long it took, to hear how she would defend herself, but when an answer came, it wasn't from my mother.

"Sometimes people can't see." Marissa ran a nervous hand through her hair and fixed her eyes on me. "Like you," she said, clasping her hands in front of her chest and rocking forward slightly. "I miss you getting up before I go to school, and I miss you at my dance recitals. I miss all the things we used to do together as a family. I don't think you're trying to hurt me. I don't think you even know you are. But you are."

For an instant I felt a white-hot anger, but it dissipated before it really even began. Marissa's eyes, discomfiting in their intensity, remained on me while I attempted to gather my thoughts. I couldn't refute what she had said. I had spent the night facing the truth about myself, and as difficult as it was to hear, Marissa was only validating what I already knew to be true. To deny it would have been enacting the same sin I accused my mother of committing, and I'd spent enough years doing that.

I, too, had followed the destructive pattern of my family, as Marissa had so succinctly pointed out. With that reminder in front of me, I couldn't very well cast stones. When thinking of the words of Horace, I'd overlooked the fact that the daughter one day becomes the mother, from guiltless to guilty. As much as I wanted to punish my mother in that moment, I forced myself to retreat.

"You're right," I told Marissa. "I have a lot of things to work on. I spent all night thinking just that. It won't be easy, but I'm determined to do it. I hope you and Matthew, and your father, can forgive me and give me another chance. I also hope we can end this terrible cycle once and for all." I turned back to my mother. "I'm sorry," I said. "I shouldn't have spoken to you like that. That's not why I came. Can we move on, for now?"

She nodded, and I was struck by how frail she looked. "You've a right to your questions, you and Naomi both, but I don't know as I have the answers," she said. "I've spent many a day the last twenty-seven years wantin' to know why you left. Now I have some idea, and I reckon knowin' somethin' is better than knowin' nothin'. The one thing I told myself when I had babies was I didn't want to suffocate you all like was done to me. It may not seem like it, but I tried to do right by you children. I did, Beth."

Another sentiment I could identify with. I was beginning to see that my mother and I had some things in common. "I was unhappy as a child," I said. "You know that. I didn't feel cared for, not by either of you. Maybe I was wrong in that; I don't know. I do know if Matthew or Marissa ever left me the way I left you, it would destroy me. I'm sorry for having put you through it. Please know my goal wasn't to hurt you; it was to save us. I had wanted to save Luke, too, but ..." I closed my eyes against the memory, a futile exercise, I knew.

"What happened to him, Beth?" She leaned back in her chair and Naomi took her hand again. "Tell me what happened to Luke."

"Do you need to rest first?" I asked her.

She shook her head, impatient. "I'll rest when you're finished tellin' me."

"You said you knew where Luke had gone," I prompted. "Did you know when he returned?"

"No." She paused to blow her nose with the tissue Naomi handed her. "When Luke stepped outside the door with your daddy, that was the last time I saw him alive."

Unlike my mother, I knew exactly when Luke had rurned. After all, I'd been waiting for him.

Chapter 30

Beth Pritchett Sloan

Luke had to come home sometime. This is what I told myself as Naomi and I turned in for the night, opening the window not only to the hope of a breeze, but to the swarm of mosquitos that had taken up residence on our bank by the creek. It was a wretchedly hot summer, and it had been a particularly trying day. The persistent whine of the tiny insects did nothing to improve my mood.

I was frustrated, I remember, not only by the heat and the barrage of gnats and mosquitos, but because I was by that time nearly eighteen years old, and I wholeheartedly resented spending my summer vacation in a scraggly cornfield at the bottom of a mountain. My hands were blistered from the constant hoeing, my back sore from pulling weeds too stubborn to submit to the blunted instrument. I was sunburned, hurting, and irritable, and by that time I had surely learned my hard work would in no way benefit me.

I wouldn't see payment in the form of either school supplies or money, nor could I bask in parental praise of a job well done. No, I had spent ten hours of backbreaking labor that day solely to avoid the consequences of refusal. I was not only frustrated, I was seething with anger, although I don't think I realized the depth of it at that time. Even worse, I saw no escape from my circumstances. I would graduate from the little red brick schoolhouse down in the village in the upcoming year, but unlike some of my classmates, I was not making plans for college. College seemed out of my reach back then, something for rich kids, smart kids, kids who weren't Pritchetts.

I know better now, of course, now that I have one child in college and another one already making plans. Rarely does a day go by that our mailbox isn't filled with shiny brochures and overstuffed envelopes from colleges and universities across the country. Mark and Matthew spent many evenings poring over the range of options available to a kid with Matt's SAT scores. As far as college was concerned, for our children it wasn't a matter of *if*, but *where*. Mark had insisted we open college accounts for both of our children as soon as they were born.

When I was Matthew's age, I had no such resources, nor did I have any inkling that scholarships and grants existed specifically for children in my situation. Given the financial circumstances of my family, I must surely have qualified for financial aid. It's quite possible I wouldn't have had to pay anything out of pocket, but I didn't know that at the time. Besides, finances were only a small part of what kept me from considering college; the bigger barrier was mental. People in my family simply didn't go to college. Continuing school past the age of high school graduation was an alien concept to me, something *other* people did, people who were as foreign to me as if descended from a different species.

I could see no way out of Cedar Hollow, no escape route to lead me away from the banks of Rugged Creek and the smell of rotting corn. That sense of hopelessness had grown steadily over the past few months as the future loomed ahead of me with no clear answers in sight. In spite of the turmoil I was feeling, I was determined not to let my somber mood ruin Luke's special day.

I was happy for him during that final dinner in our shabby kitchen. I really was. Seated around the laminate-topped table with the mismatched chairs, I enjoyed watching him open his gift. I was glad my mother had found a way to purchase the knife he'd admired for months, and I ate the cake along with everyone else, enjoying its moist richness. Even our father was uncharacteristically agreeable, proud, perhaps, that his only son was reaching adulthood, next in line to take over the delusional

Pritchett Empire. As far as our family dinners went, it was remarkably peaceful.

After our father took Luke away and Naomi and I finished cleaning the kitchen, we spent the remainder of the evening playing chess at the kitchen table, too drained of energy by the heat to do much of anything else. I think both of us were also hoping to remain awake long enough to hear Luke bounding up the porch steps, eager to tell us about his night by the fire. By ten o'clock, bored with chess and lacking the initiative to find anything else to do, we gave up on Luke, and following our mother's example, retired to our room for an early bedtime.

"When do you think Luke will come home?" Naomi asked, yawning, as we turned down the faded sheet in preparation for another restless night's sleep.

"Hopefully soon," I said. I think both of us were worried about him, neither of us trusting him to make safe decisions among the whiskey-drinking men in the woods, and both of us knowing the men certainly wouldn't be looking out for him. I considered creeping down the path to spy on them, but quickly rejected the idea. There was nothing I could do, particularly since Luke *wanted* to be with them. I doubted very much he would willingly sneak back home with me. And the chance of getting caught—and what that might mean for me—was simply too great.

Naomi fell asleep quickly, but I remained awake, my body exhausted to the core, my mind still bitterly reflecting on my day in the cornfield. I could not find a path to a future for myself outside of Cedar Hollow, yet I also couldn't imagine living out my life at the shack on Rugged Creek. Would I be twenty, thirty, and still following my father's orders, day in and day out, at the mercy of his belt? After tossing and turning for an eternity, I gave in to the impulse to get up, leaving the damp sheets and stale house behind in search of a breeze from the creek. I wanted to be alone with my thoughts, none of which were comforting, but all of which needed to be examined.

It was there that Luke found me, literally stumbling over me. I'd heard him coming for some time, torn between amusement and alarm at the slurred words of the song he sang tunelessly as he picked his way towards me down the bank. He'd clearly stayed true to his word, joining the men in passing the bottle. I managed to scoot out of the way just before he hit the ground, his hands wildly grappling for some sort of hold as he fell.

"Back so soon?" I asked, grinning down at him as he rolled over and struggled to sit up.

"Beth? What're you doing out here?" He pushed the hair out of his eyes and squinted at me before holding his prized possession aloft for me to view in the light of the moon. "Look what I got. And they refilled it for me, too," he said, as he struggled to remove the cork.

"Let me help," I said, reaching for the bottle. "And let's walk. You need some air." My hope was to distract Luke from the bottle while simultaneously helping him sober up. I didn't know about alcohol poisoning back then, but I remembered my own experience vividly, and I hadn't had nearly the amount to drink Luke supposedly had. I knew at the very least he would be horribly sick the next morning. I was not as demonstrative as Luke and Naomi—I was not openly affectionate—but I did love my baby brother, and I was worried about him. We set off towards the bridge, our best option for catching a breeze. Luke shuffled along beside me and I put an arm around him to steady him.

"Where's the bottle?" he asked, lurching against me, and I shoved it quickly into the back pocket of my jeans.

"I'm getting it," I lied. "The cork is stuck, so give me a minute." Luke grumbled but didn't argue. "Tell me how it went," I said, hoping to divert his attention from the wretched drink. "What did they do? Did they talk to you?"

Thankfully, Luke seemed eager to tell me about his experience at the fire. As he told me how he'd taken his first drink—to hoots of approval from the men of the family—I steered him to the dirt road that led to the bridge. "Careful,

Luke," I said, guiding him to sit on the side as we always had, legs dangling, arms propped against the rail. "Hopefully it'll be cooler up here. Feel the breeze?"

"Nope," Luke said, swaying and patting his cheeks. "I can't even feel my face. Beth, I think I'm going to be sick."

I helped him lean over the rail and held him steady as he emptied the contents of his stomach into the creek. "Lie down," I told him when he'd finished, pulling him gently onto his back on the wooden planks of the bridge. Rarely was there traffic on the bridge. Very few people lived outside of town—most who did were relatives who unfortunately had no intention of leaving our property anytime soon—and folks from town had no desire to visit among the Pritchetts. Even those few who kept my family in business knew better than to approach the Pritchett clan uninvited, particularly late at night, lest they come face to face with the barrel of a gun.

"I'm going to get some water for you," I said. "Don't move, understand?"

Luke made no answer except to groan, and I turned to go, jogging down the dark bank to the edge of the creek. Once there, I hesitated briefly, then emptied the liquor onto the bank and rinsed out the bottle before filling it with cold, clear water. I had been tempted, it's true. A part of me wanted to save Luke's liquor for myself. I longed for the burning in my throat, the warmth in my stomach. I wanted to drink just enough to forget the troubling thoughts spinning through my mind. But I wanted even more to help Luke.

I hurried back to find him flat on his back, the moonlight on his face. His arms and legs were splayed wide, and he was snoring in true Pritchett fashion. At that moment I could see both sides of Luke, as if looking through a portal. I saw our sweet Luke, the boy who made us laugh, who made us shake our heads with a grudging admiration for his antics, the boy who loved us and worked hard to protect us in whatever small ways he could.

But I also saw the man he might become—would surely become, because what choice did he have? I saw him aging before my eyes, his innate recklessness unchecked, his impulsive desire for adventure leading him down the path of our father and his father before him. I saw for Luke the same hopeless future I saw for me, and it was unacceptable.

I sat beside him and dampened my shirttail with water, patting it lightly across his face to cool him. He didn't stir, so I leaned back against the rail beside him, tilting my head to gaze at the stars as if they might provide the answers I sought. I knew I had no chance of waking him, and I certainly couldn't carry him. Even at thirteen, he was taller and stronger than I. Instead, I would watch over him through the night, and in the morning I would tell them—all of them—*enough*. And then I would leave, taking my siblings with me. I didn't know where we would go or how we would survive. I didn't even know how we'd make it out of Cedar Hollow without facing the rage of our father. I only knew that if we wanted any chance at all for a normal life, we had no choice but to go.

Chapter 31

Naomi Pritchett Wells

My heart ached as I sat across from Beth and listened to her story. Many of her memories mirrored my own, but the ones specific to her were painful for me to hear, not just because they hurt her, but because of the *aloneness* she must have felt. Beth and I shared everything in those days. As small as our house was, we had no choice, but as all people do, we kept some thoughts secret even from each other, perhaps from guilt or embarrassment, or—more likely—because our private thoughts were literally all we owned. Yet, I couldn't help but feel guilty for not having known the extent of the pain that she'd felt.

"Do you remember," she asked, looking at me, "what happened the next morning?"

I remembered that, too. I had awakened to my father's angry voice. Something had happened with one of the stills, some sort of explosion, not a very big one, apparently, but Uncle Wayne had been hurt. It wasn't unheard of for there to be trouble with the stills, but aside from a nasty incident long before I was born involving Papaw Pritchett's sister-in-law, no real harm had ever come of one.

That particular incident had caused third degree burns over most of the poor woman's upper body and would have led to the end of the Pritchett whiskey business had Great-Aunt Bernice not stuck to her story of tripping and falling into the cast iron laundry kettle, which was hanging atop the outdoor fire pit over a smoldering fire. In spite of the horrendous weeks of pain she endured before succumbing to her injuries, she never did change her story, and for that she had become a legend within the Pritchett family history, held forth as an example of what it meant to be included into the Pritchett family business.

Hearing that story as a child, I had wondered what, exactly, it *did* mean to be included into the Pritchett family business. My father spoke of Great-Aunt Bernice with a sort of reverence, but given the oft-shared graphic descriptions of her injuries, I thought the woman would have been better off trading whatever misplaced sense of pride she felt at upholding the Pritchett family code of honor for a *different* family, one void of temperamental contraptions—not to mention people—with a tendency to explode.

At any rate, the morning before our lives changed, I ran to the window, morbidly curious as to the severity of Uncle Wayne's injuries. I watched as my father loaded him into the back of the truck, cursing angrily and directing him to tell anyone who asked that he'd been careless with gasoline while burning a pile of trash. I wasn't sure if my father was angry because of the unwanted attention Uncle Wayne's injuries might bring to the family, or because Uncle Wayne would clearly be out of commission for some time to come. I don't suppose it mattered, and knowing my father as I did, I was scarcely surprised by his lack of empathy for his wounded younger brother.

Uncle Wayne's face was red and blistered, I remember, and I could see translucent pieces of skin hanging from his hands as he held them aloft. He was making an awful sound, something between a moan and a cry, and my mother climbed into the bed of the truck to see to him, her arms full of rags and a bowl of ice, before my father sped off down the mountain, his reckless maneuvering over potholes and tree roots exhibiting little concern for the passengers carelessly tossed about in the back.

I ran outside in search of either Luke or Beth, eager to get their thoughts on what had just transpired, but I could find neither of them. In fact, the entire place was eerily quiet, my army of relatives no doubt having vacated the property in lieu of a possible, albeit unlikely, visit from Officer Wimbley, the lone deputy assigned to Cedar Hollow at that time. As it turned out, Officer Wimbley did pay a visit that evening, but by the time he was summoned, the exploded still, and Uncle Wayne's resultant injuries, were scarcely remembered.

I wandered about for a while, half-heartedly looking for my siblings before giving up and returning to the house. I was annoyed they hadn't waited for me before taking off on whatever venture they'd decided to pursue, but the day was unbearably hot, and I wasn't motivated or irritated enough to continue my search. Instead, I lounged on the couch, enjoying my unexpected day off from whatever chores my father might have assigned. A day of leisure was unheard of for us, and I couldn't recall ever having had the place to myself before that day. I flipped through old magazines, ate leftovers from the refrigerator, and painted my nails with the frosted pink polish Beth had brought home from the diner, another gift from Kay Langley.

It was well after noon when Beth finally returned from wherever she'd been, and I was surprised to see her alone. "Where's Luke?" I asked, looking up from my prone position on the couch, where I'd directed our only fan to sweep over me during the heat of the day—something I'd never have dared to do had my parents been home. I'd expected a smart remark upon being discovered by one of my siblings, and I'd readied my own response in anticipation: *If you'd bothered to talk to me before disappearing, I'd have invited you to share in my day of relaxation.* But not only did Beth not remark on the nail polish and pile of magazines on the arm of the couch, she also didn't answer my question. "Where's Luke?" I asked her again.

She shrugged but didn't speak, and for a moment I wondered if I had done something to anger her and Luke. After all, not only had they taken off without me, my sister was now apparently not speaking to me. But as I looked at her, I intuited that whatever the problem was, it wasn't me. Judging by her appearance, the day had not been an enjoyable one for her, certainly not as relaxing as the one I'd had by myself at the house. She looked awful. She was filthy, and her arms and legs were scraped and bleeding.

She didn't look at me as she passed by, her head lowered, a tangle of unkempt hair hiding her face from me. She went into our bedroom and closed the door without a word. I let her go, assuming our uncle's injuries had more deeply affected her than they had me. I felt momentarily ashamed of myself for painting my nails and flipping through magazines while Uncle Wayne was undoubtedly suffering. We stayed that way, me overcome by guilt on the couch, and Beth alone in our room, until we heard our father's truck straining up the mountain and I had to scramble to return the fan to its usual place and clean up the mess I'd made.

Uncle Wayne was taken to the hospital in Huntington, my father said, filling us in as our relatives returned to their encampments in our yard as if summoned by an invisible force. He'd be fine, my father told us, but he'd have to stay there for a while. "Which means," he said, scanning the assembled family for Luke, "we're all going to have to step in to do his work for the next few weeks, especially you, Luke. You're old enough." He paused, craning his head from side to side. "Damn it, where the hell is Luke?" he asked, looking to Beth and me for the answer.

"I haven't seen him all day," I said, while beside me Beth remained mute.

"Well he needs to get his ass back here," said my father. "I'm not in the mood for his hijinks today; we got too much going on for that sort of foolishness. Y'all go find him right now, and tell him to get back here before I get my belt."

We hurried to warn Luke, not only Beth and me, but our cousins as well. None of us, I'd thought at the time, wanting him to have to face our father and his belt. Of course, I understood now that Beth had known all along where we'd find him.

"You sent our cousins up the mountain," I said, "in the wrong direction. I wanted to come with you, but you didn't want me to. When I refused to leave, you made me stay behind you." The black cherry tree outside my mother's window cast shadows across the woven rug of Erma Puckett's boarding home floor as I struggled to understand. "You wanted to go back to him at the creek." I shivered as the truth dawned on me. "You knew exactly where to go, and you didn't want me to see him."

Across from me, Beth nodded. "I was confused," she said. "I couldn't remember exactly what had happened. I suppose Mark would say my mind was protecting me. But I knew he was at the creek, and I knew there was something you didn't need to see."

"I don't understand," I said. "You stayed with him that night to protect him. You planned for all of us to leave the next day. What happened? If you were there when he died, why didn't you come and get help?"

"Let me finish," she said. "It isn't easy to say, and it won't be easy to hear. I'm sorry for that. I really am. But I need to tell it the way it happened."

Chapter 32

Beth Pritchett Sloan

I awakened to the sound of Luke calling my name. I had not intended to fall asleep, but after my day of work in the brutal sun, my body had simply betrayed me. I sat up quickly, searching for him. He was sitting on the railing, his back to the west, facing me, silhouetted by the moon. He swayed from side to side, clearly still under the influence of the rotgut that was the pride of my abominable family. I had no idea what time it was, other than judging it was well past midnight, given the moon at Luke's back. "Where's the bottle, Beth?" he asked, his words still faintly slurred. "You said you'd open it for me."

I struggled to wake up, staggering to my feet towards Luke, trying to get my bearings. He had no business sitting on the rail in his current state, but he lacked the judgment to understand the danger he was in. "I tried," I told him, lying. I saw no point in telling him the truth. It would only upset him. "But it wouldn't open. Besides, Luke, you've had enough. You've already been sick, and you were more or less passed out for at least a couple of hours. Let's go home, okay?" I held out my hand, beckoning him. "Let's go get some sleep away from all these godawful bugs." I swatted at one on my shoulder and another on my leg, as if to emphasize the point.

He shifted on the railing, and I gasped. "Luke, be careful. You'll fall." I took another step forward. "Come with me. It's time to go home."

"I want my bottle, Beth," he said, a hint of a whine in his voice. "Give it to me."

"No, Luke." I shook my head. "You don't need it. Now come on. Let's go." I was becoming frustrated with him, tired and sore from the long day, knowing I would face more of the same in the morning. I was also itching with mosquito bites that covered my arms and legs, even my face. I wanted to go home, and my patience with Luke was wearing thin.

"It isn't yours!" he shouted at me, and I flinched. I wasn't used to Luke shouting; none of us were. I stepped closer to him, hoping to take him by the arm, but he yanked it away. "Give it to me, Beth." He was angry, his spittle spraying my face with the force of his words. I saw our father in Luke then, more than I ever had before, and I'm pained to admit for just an instant I was repulsed by my brother. I hated what I believed he would become, hated the man I feared he would someday be, the man I saw in his face in that instant.

With some effort, I tamped down my anger, sighing with exasperation. "No, Luke. Let's talk about this tomorrow. For now, we both need to get to bed."

That's when he struck out at me. Had Luke been himself he would never, ever have struck out at any of us, not our parents, not Naomi, not me. But he wasn't himself; he was a confused thirteen-year-old boy, a boy desperate for his father's acceptance, a boy cursed with Pritchett genes and under the influence of corn liquor. Luke had always felt an affinity with the Pritchetts, and I had always felt a sense of foreboding about where that would lead him. That night, on the Rugged Creek Bridge, it took him exactly where I had feared. I dodged from his fist, and he swayed on the railing.

"Luke! Come with me. You're going to fall. Please, Luke, let me take you home." I was fraught with worry by that point.

But he didn't listen. Instead, he swung at me again. "Give me my bottle, Beth. You got no right to keep it. Daddy gave it to me. To *me*," he repeated, thumping his chest, as if he thought our father had somehow blessed him with the gift of a bottle of whiskey. I dodged again, but not quickly enough. His fist caught me on the shoulder, not hard enough to hurt me, but enough to shift his already precarious balance. In spite of that, he swung again. And out of instinct as much as anger, I swung back.

Luke's eyes grew huge as my fist connected with his chest. He tilted back, his hands scrambling for the rails. Immediately, I realized what I'd done, and I reached out to him, grabbing for his flailing arms, missing, finally managing to seize his ankle as he plunged backward over the side. Time stood still as our eyes locked, his wide and afraid, mine urgently pleading as he dangled, head down, over the creek. "Luke, grab the bridge! Pull yourself up and grab the bottom of the bridge!"

But he couldn't. I don't know if he was too panicked, or too inebriated, or perhaps simply too shocked that I had struck him in return, but for whatever reason, he couldn't seem to understand what I was telling him to do. And I couldn't hold on forever. His foot, sweaty from the humid night air, was slipping from my grasp. I dug my nails into his flesh, hugging his foot against my chest as I bent over the rail, wedging myself against the post, frantically searching for a better hold. But Luke's weight, combined with his frenzied struggling, worked against me.

The last thing I saw before losing my grip was Luke's face. Not the face of the Pritchett man I'd so worried he'd become, not the face of our father, but Luke's own dear, sweet face, completely sober in those last few seconds, fully aware of what was about to happen. "Help me, Beth," he said, and then he was gone.

I paused in my story to gaze at the three women across from me. Marissa was openly sobbing, holding the collar of her shirt over her face. My mother had her eyes closed, her hands pressed to her cheeks. And Naomi, she just looked at me with tears in her eyes. I could see by her expression she was sorry, but for whom I didn't know.

What I didn't tell them was that I heard Luke hit the rocks below. There was no initial splash, just the horrible sound of impact before he slipped silently into the water. On one level I must have known, even as I screamed his name, that he was gone.

What I also didn't tell them was that sometimes, during my late night sojourns at the front window with my bottle of wine, I wondered if I could have held on longer. I had been repulsed by Luke's resemblance to my father in those last moments, it's true. But I loved my brother, and I knew the boy striking out at me wasn't really Luke. I did know that, and I held on as long as I possibly could. Didn't I?

Chapter 33

Beth Pritchett Sloan

"It was an accident," Naomi said, as if reading my thoughts. She reached across to me, and I took her hand gratefully. Naomi had always comforted me, and I had always needed it. We hadn't changed much, Naomi and me. For that, I was thankful.

"It was," I agreed, "but there are so many things I could have done differently."

"Like what, Beth?" she asked. "There are things all of us could have done differently, but would it have mattered? You were just a girl. You couldn't have changed the trajectory of our family." Next to her, our mother studied her hands in silence, and I wondered what she was thinking. Was she blaming me?

Like what, Naomi had asked, the question that had tormented me for decades. The memory of Luke's death, as well as the events leading up to it, had been an albatross about my neck the majority of my life. Perhaps, with the telling of my story, like Coleridge's *Mariner*, I might find some purpose, or maybe even absolution. At the very least, I hoped to find some peace.

I had run immediately to the creek bank, not pausing to remove my shoes before plunging into the water, tripping over exposed rocks and mountain debris in a futile effort to save Luke. I knew he couldn't be saved; I'd seen him as he fell. Even worse, I'd heard the force with which he'd landed. On one level, I knew he was gone, but on another, I refused to accept it.

At first, I couldn't find him. In spite of the soft light the moon cast upon the night, I was unable to distinguish between shadow and true form. Every shadow seemed, to me, to encompass the form of a boy, and I splashed maniacally from one to the other, cutting myself on the rocks, entangling myself in water grasses, in a desperate search for my brother.

I saw the rock on which he'd landed, a ridiculously innocent looking boulder, as they all were when the water was high. But the water wasn't high, the end result of which a rock scarcely larger than a breadbox could transform into a potentially deadly weapon. I also saw the mark Luke's body had made on it, the dark patch glistening in the light of the moon, and I turned my head from the confirmation of his death. I could not bear to look and would not accept the evidence.

I don't know how long I thrashed about the creek in my desperate search for Luke. What I do know is that the first light of dawn had touched the sky before I found him. He was wedged underneath the bridge, carried by the current and caught between rocks and a support beam. His foot was what I saw first, bobbing with the flow. His upper body was below the water, and I dove for him in a frenzied attempt to bring him to the surface and allow him to breathe.

I wasn't functioning rationally, but I didn't realize that at the time. My one and only thought was to bring Luke's head above water. In spite of the evidence around me, in spite of the time elapsed from the moment of his fall, I thought if I could just rescue his face from the freezing waters of the creek, he would be okay.

I can hear Mark in my head with the telling of the story, and I know what he would have said: *Shock. You were in shock, Beth. You'd just witnessed your brother's death.* And no doubt I *was* in shock. My memories occurred in jumbled fragments: a picture, a sound, a thought, a world of sensations without reason. None of it made sense, not then, and not now.

Time and again, I held my breath and plunged under water, lying on the bottom of the shallow bed, struggling to free his torso from the unyielding beam. *The water's not deep*, I remember pleading with Luke. *Get up! You have to get up. The water's not deep. Just raise your head! For Pete's sake, Luke, just raise your head!* When he wouldn't listen, I grew angry. *Dammit, Luke, help me get you out of here!*

I have only the vaguest memory of what happened next. At some point I realized the sun was up, blinding me with its reflection on the water. I remember hearing our father's truck as it rumbled across the bridge. Later I learned he'd been taking Uncle Wayne to the hospital, but I didn't know that at the time. Had I been in my right mind, I like to think I would have run after him, flagging him down to help us. But I wasn't in my right mind. All I could think at the time was if Luke and I didn't get out of the creek and back to the house, Daddy would beat us for sure.

I may have slept at some point, propped unsteadily against the boulders by Luke's side. I remember being cold, unbearably cold, and worrying that Luke would become hypothermic if I couldn't get him out of the creek soon. I hadn't yet accepted that he was dead; shock kept me deep in denial. I was still convinced if I could just get him out of the water, everything would be fine.

"I don't remember walking home," I said, "but I do remember seeing you, Naomi. You were in the living room, lying on the couch. I knew I had something to tell you, but everything was foggy. I couldn't make my mouth form the words, and I wasn't even sure what words it needed to form.

"The next thing I recall is Daddy telling us to go find Luke. That's when I remembered he was at the creek. At first I was irritated, anticipating an argument with him: *I told you we'd get the belt if we didn't hurry up and get home! I told you to come on!* But on another level, I knew something was wrong, and I didn't want you to see it. For the life of me, I couldn't put the pieces together, not until we'd made our way back to the creek and I saw Luke again. That's when it finally became real for me."

Chapter 34

Naomi Pritchett Wells

I remembered Beth's screams as if it were yesterday. They echoed through my head, and as I had all those years ago, I covered my ears, shrinking from the sound. Relatives had come running even before we'd made it back to the house, summoned by the sound of her cries. Given what I'd just learned, I suppose something must have broken for Beth when she'd returned to Luke's body, the ugly truth finally forcing its way through her denial. I didn't know what had happened, at first—none of us did, until my mother shook Beth by the shoulders, finally slapping her and demanding to know what all the ruckus was about.

Even then, Beth didn't speak. Sobbing, averting her face, she gestured towards the creek. I couldn't see what she was pointing at, but my mother could, and her own wail of grief picked up where Beth's had left off.

Before I could move in for a better look, my father ordered me to take the younger cousins to the house, not out of any sense of concern for their wellbeing, but because they were underfoot and in the way, their curiosity, like mine, propelling them towards the creek bank. "Get them the hell out of here," he'd said. "Ain't none of us got time for them right now."

Reluctantly, I led them to the house, where we waited for what seemed hours but couldn't have been more than a few minutes, for someone to tell us what was going on. Uncle Bobby's wife, Aunt Babe, was the one who finally broke the news by way of ordering me to call the sheriff. "Tell him to get on out here," she yelled through the open doorway. "Luke's dead up under the bridge."

At first I thought I'd misheard her, and I hesitated. Luke couldn't possibly be dead. Just the night before he'd winked at me on his way out the door. "Are you deaf, child?" Aunt Babe's voice cut through my confusion. "I told you to call the damn sheriff. Now get your ass in gear."

The next few days blended together. Like Beth, I remember snippets of sound: my mother crying, my aunts barking orders. I remember snapshots: my uncles huddled together outside the kitchen window, my younger cousins seated together on the couch, eyes wide and afraid. I remember being ordered to keep an eye on them. They were uncharacteristically subdued, their faces displaying the same confused expression I saw on my own in the cloudy mirror over the dressing table in my shared room with Beth.

I remember the morning of the funeral and Beth's refusal of my hand. I remember my mother's back as she closed her bedroom door. I remember the never-ending evening stretching out before us, as Beth and I cleaned the kitchen and waited for neighbors and relatives to leave us alone for the night.

I remember the stifling heat of our bedroom, and Beth's face in its intensity as she asked me to run away with her. Finally, I remember boarding the train, watching Cedar Hollow recede into the distance as I went in search of a breath of fresh air. I had not realized the finality of my actions that morning, had certainly not known the magnitude of all I was throwing away: my childhood, my family, my home. It was too much. All I'd wanted was to breathe.

I hadn't known I was crying until I felt my mother's hand on my cheek, her fingers rough against my skin. "Let's rest now, Naomi," she said, and I nodded, exhausted. I was overwhelmed with sadness for all of us, but underneath it, I also felt a stirring of hope. Maybe it could be laid to rest now. Maybe we could make a fresh start. I hoped so. More than anything, I wanted my family in my life. I hadn't realized the extent of the loss until now, but having discovered what was missing, I couldn't bear the thought of losing it again.

"This is a lot to take in without havin' any sleep," my mother was saying. She turned to Beth. "We'll meet again this evenin', but for now, I think we all need a little rest."

She struggled to her feet and went to Beth, placing a hand on her head before leaning down to brush a kiss against her cheek. I couldn't remember my mother ever kissing us, certainly not Beth, who had shunned any show of affection from her. I was pleased to see Beth accept her kiss without comment before standing to leave, her arm tightly around Marissa. Marissa spared me a sad smile before returning her mother's embrace and closing the door quietly behind them.

My mother was right; we all needed a little rest, but I found myself too tired to stand, and like the little girl who used to knock on her door at night, I craved my mother's company. She must have sensed what I was feeling, because after switching off the lamp and closing the blinds, she tucked the afghan firmly around my shoulders before leaning down to kiss my cheek, as well. Then I slept.

Chapter 35

Marissa Elizabeth Sloan

It looked exactly the way I had imagined it. "Can we go inside?" I asked my mom, who had stopped on the pathway, frowning. I knew it couldn't have been easy for her to take me to their old house by the creek. After everything she'd told us that morning, I understood why she had such bad memories of the place, and I was surprised she had suggested it.

As soon as we'd stepped into the hall outside Nana's room, Mom had surrounded me in a huge hug. Usually, I would have tried to break away after a second or two—I don't really like being squeezed for too long—but this time I hugged her back, and I didn't let go until after she did. It was weird to think before our trip to West Virginia, I hadn't really known anything about her at all. The things I'd just learned helped me to understand her better. I felt sad for her.

She blamed herself for Luke dying, but it wasn't her fault. She had tried to do the right thing, and I was proud of her for that. I understood Luke's death and my mother's drinking were connected. I guess she was trying to forget what had happened, but with everything I'd learned, I was more worried than ever. After hearing so much about my mom's family history, I wondered if she would really be able to quit. I hoped so. I really wanted things to get better for us at home.

"Are you okay?" I asked her as I hugged her close.

"I am," she answered, stroking my back. "I feel as if a huge weight has been lifted. I'm not sure where we go from here, but it has to be better than where we've been." She squeezed me again before letting go and stepping back. "Are you tired?" she asked, brushing back my hair.

I guess I must have been the only one who actually slept through the night, because I wasn't tired at all. I was looking forward to exploring the town and the mountain trails, and that's what I told my mom.

I was surprised when she agreed with me. "How would you like to see where I grew up?" she asked. I could hardly believe it. I had wanted to ask her to take me there, but I'd been afraid she'd say no. I was feeling closer to my mom that I could remember feeling in years. It was important to me to see where she'd lived. I wanted to see the places she'd talked about, the roof they'd slept on during the floods, the porch where Naomi and Luke had waited up for my mom, the bedroom she'd shared with Aunt Naomi. I wanted to be able to match the stories I'd heard with the places they'd happened.

"Are you sure?" I asked. "You're really okay with taking me there?"

Mom smiled. "I'm fine, Marissa. Really. I feel better than I've felt in a long, long time."

We had taken our time, following the creek past the bridge where Aunt Naomi and I had met Mom earlier. I couldn't help looking at the rocks in a different way, after hearing what had happened to my Uncle Luke. I also couldn't imagine what Mom must have felt that night. I tried not to think too much about it; it was just too sad, and I wanted to enjoy my time with my mom.

It was hot outside, much hotter than when I'd walked the same path with Aunt Naomi that morning, and the bugs were out, flying around my face and buzzing into my ears. Bug spray, I thought to myself. I was still excited about exploring the trails, but next time I'd come prepared. I already took for granted there would be a next time. I walked in the creek again, splashing myself to cool off, but Mom stayed on the bank.

After a little while, she left the bank and turned right, following a path I wouldn't have even noticed, it was so choked out with vines. We didn't talk much. I wasn't sure what to say to her, and besides, she didn't seem to want to talk. I think she'd even forgotten I was there. It wasn't one of our angry silences, though; it was peaceful. When we came to the clearing just a few feet in I had to repeat my question. "Mom? Can we go inside?"

"I don't know if that's a good idea," she finally answered, staring at the house in front of us. "Be careful, Marissa. This house wasn't in the best of shape when I was your age. I hate to think how unstable it is now. Not to mention, it's been abandoned for over a year. There's no telling what sorts of wildlife may have taken up residence."

From where we were standing, I could see the tin roof my mom had talked about, rusted all the way through in some places. Paint was peeling off the slats of the wall facing us, and I couldn't tell what color it had once been—something light, maybe even white. There were two windows, both broken, and I knew from my mom's stories the one on the left led to the room she shared with Naomi, while the one on the right, over the sagging porch, led to the living room. There was a wooden swing, peeling with the same color paint as the house. One of the chains had either broken or come unhooked, so that half the swing was suspended in the air while the other half rested on the porch.

Huge trees surrounded the little house, blocking out the sun. I couldn't believe the change in temperature; without the sun shining down on us, the air was chilly. I shivered, wishing I hadn't gotten quite so wet in the creek. I don't know if it felt gloomy to me because of the shadows, or because of the things I knew had happened there.

I wouldn't have admitted it to my mom, but it felt haunted to me, like at any minute I might see my Uncle Luke walking towards us with a fishing pole. I'd heard so much about him by then I could see him clearly: tall and thin, strong and tanned, barefoot and shirtless, with cut-off blue jean shorts and the trademark Pritchett curls, dark and wild around his head. "Marissa!" he'd call to me. "Want to go fishin'?" And I would, because although I hadn't known it until then, a part of me—the Pritchett part, I guess—wanted to experience running through the dark woods, gigging frogs and catching fish, sleeping on a tin roof and telling stories under the stars.

I almost expected to hear the voices of the relatives Mom said were always hanging out in the yard. That thought made me shiver again. I wanted to know more about my mom, but the idea of running into a bunch of drunk people this far from civilization made me nervous, even if they were my family. What was I saying? *Especially* if they were my family.

"Where are the stills?" I asked my mom. I hadn't meant to whisper, but somehow it came out that way.

She pointed past the house. "Back there, down a path into the trees. But they won't be there now. Kay said they stopped making whiskey shortly after we left. I doubt there's anything left of the stills, especially not with copper selling the way it does. If my family didn't sell it, someone else would have."

I was relieved to hear that, but still a little spooked by the place. It was so easy to picture little kids running through the yard, half naked, with dirty faces and tangled hair. I could see women running after them, yelling directions and swatting bottoms. In my imagination, men sprawled under trees and on stumps, pints in hand, swigging the afternoon away. It was like something from a movie, but it was also my heritage. I felt confused by it all, sort of longing for it, but at the same time a little afraid of what it meant.

Mom must have sensed what I was feeling, because she looked at me and smiled. "There were good things about this place, too," she said. "It wasn't so dark and overgrown when we were kids." She moved forward on the path, and I followed. "That spot"—she pointed to the roof as we drew closer—"over on the right. See how it's nearly collapsed? That's where we camped during the floods. No doubt we're responsible for the shape it's in now. We had some of the best times up there." She smiled at the memory. "You can see the creek from the roof," she continued, "but of course most of the times we were up there, our *yard* was the creek."

I followed her up what was left of the trail, all the way to the front steps. "Be careful," she said. "The rails are wobbly. They always were."

We climbed slowly up the few steps, me holding tight to the rail, because as wobbly as it was, the steps were even worse. Mom crossed the porch, the wooden slats creaking under her feet, and tried the door. "Locked," she said. "We can probably get a key from my mother." She moved to look through the busted living room window. "There's nothing here. She must have taken what she could use and tossed the rest. It was all junk, anyway. Be careful; there's still some glass in the frame."

She moved aside to let me look, but there wasn't much to see. The room was empty. The ceiling and walls were dingy and stained with watermarks, the wooden floor faded and scuffed. Overhead, a bird flapped across the empty room, and I jumped. Like my mom had said, wildlife had started to move in. Across the dark room I could see a doorway into what must have been the kitchen. It was empty, too, but I could see the spaces where the refrigerator and stove used to be. I could also see what looked like a nest of some sort—mice, maybe, or squirrels—spilling out from the cabinet underneath the kitchen sink. What I really wanted to see was the room she shared with Aunt Naomi, but there was too much glass to take a chance of climbing through the broken window, and I was a little afraid of what we might run into.

"If you really want to look, we can get the key from my mother and come back tomorrow," my mom said. "That way, Matthew and your dad can come with us. We can even pick up a couple of machetes from the store and go back to where the stills used to be, if you're interested." I turned to see her smiling.

"Matthew and Dad are coming here?" I asked, afraid I hadn't heard her right. That would be awesome, if they really were coming. I couldn't wait to show Matthew the creek, and I really wanted to see where the stills had been. I wanted to see everything. I felt drawn to the place, as if I belonged to it in some way. I know that sounds crazy, but that's how I felt. "Tomorrow?" I asked, hoping that was what she'd said.

"Tomorrow," she confirmed. "I have to pick them up bright and early, at seven. I called your dad from the bridge this morning, before you and Aunt Naomi showed up. He was going to call Matthew to see if he could take a couple of days away from school. Matt texted their flight information when we were on our way back to the boarding home. I want us all here together. Marissa," she said, taking me by the shoulders, turning me to face her. "I love you and Matt, and your dad. I really want us to fix things. I'm going to try really hard."

"I will too, Mom," I told her, and I meant it. I knew I wasn't always easy to get along with. I'd been mad at my mom for years. Sometimes the only way for me to get back at her was to give her a hard time, but I thought maybe knowing about her past would help me have more patience with her. I swatted at a bug that seemed determined to land on my eyeball. "Bug spray," I said. "We need machetes and bug spray. Then we'll be ready."

She laughed, and it was good to hear. I couldn't remember the last time I'd heard my mom's real laugh. "You've discovered the secret to survival in the mountains," she said. "Now let's get out of here. This place feels haunted. I keep expecting Luke to show up any minute with a fishing pole."

Chapter 36

Geraldine Porter Pritchett

I watch my girl sleep for the first time in longer than I care to remember. She's still a pretty thing, tucked up under the afghan with her hands under her cheek like she used to do when she was little. It's hard for me to believe she's as old as she is. Why, I was younger than she is now when she left me.

I know I should rest too, but I had that nap earlier and my head is spinning too much to allow me another one. Instead, I grab an afghan of my own, and settle in the chair next to Naomi's, reaching out to pat her while she sleeps. I wish Beth was still here, resting with us, all of us peaceful in the cool, dark room, but she's a good momma, better than I ever was, and I'm hoping she's taking some time to fix things with Marissa. I see the trouble brewing between them, and I don't like it one bit. We need to end this foolishness right here and now, all of it: the hard feelings and resentments and bitterness. It's near about destroyed us all, from generation to generation. That's enough of that.

I wish my Luke was here, too. Not a day has gone by all these years that I haven't grieved the loss of my boy. He feels particularly close to me today. I can almost see him next to me, watching us get this mess settled once and for all. I think he'd like what's happening here. Luke didn't like squabbles; he was my peacemaker, Luke was. He was the one always trying to tease Beth out of her dark moods, always trying to cover for Naomi and protect her from her daddy.

I don't feel Junior here, but knowing Junior the way I do, that don't surprise me none. Junior wasn't keen on forgiveness; he didn't hand it out, and he never thought to ask for it. Beth accused her daddy and me of some terrible things, some of them expected, others not, but all of them true. And I see from the telling she was right: I did kill Luke, as surely as if I'd pushed him off that bridge myself. That's a hard truth to swallow, but there it is.

I wish I had the answers as to the *why* of everything, but I don't. I can look back now and see plain as day all the things that went wrong, but for the life of me, I couldn't see it when I was there living it. It occurs to me I spent the better part of my life feeling aggrieved at my own parents, on account of the way they raised me. Ain't that a foolish way to have spent my short time on this earth? All I ended up doing was bringing the poison into my own house and spreading it to my children.

But we're going to get it all worked out. I know we are, because I'm going to tell them how sorry I am for my failings and ask for their forgiveness. I think they'll give it to me, too. My daughters are better than I am, and if they forget that, all they have to do is look at me to see what happens when you live a vexed life. And I know they don't want to be like me.

Chapter 37

Kay Langley

Friday nights are always busy at my diner, but Lord have mercy, that night was something else. I hadn't no sooner got one family seated before another one showed up, and I'll tell you what, by seven o'clock that evening it looked to me like at least a hundred of the two-hundred-sixteen people living in Cedar Hollow was seated at my tables. Andrew was on the grill but Teresa, bless her heart, was about to pop if she didn't deliver soon. Andrew and me had ordered her off her feet.

That left just Riva and me working the tables, until Opal and Richard Huffman showed up from the children's lodge. They'd made a habit of taking dinner with me on Friday evenings. I would have thought by then, after waiting on kids all week long, they'd be ready to sit down and get waited on themselves, but not that night. "Where's your aprons?" Opal asked, as soon as she saw how hard me and Riva was working. I tried to wave her off, but she wouldn't have none of it. Before I knew what was happening, Richard was back in the kitchen helping Andrew, and Opal was seating Corinne Johnson and Jessie at a table Riva'd just cleared in the back corner.

I felt bad, them jumping in like that, but they insisted. "Stop your worryin'," Richard told me, "We're happy to help. Besides, Jessie and Corinne are savin' us a seat for when things slow down." I quit arguing then and just enjoyed the help. Truthfully, I don't know as the three of us could've handled it without them.

I would like to take credit for the fact dang near the whole town chose my diner as their eating place that evening—after all, pot roast was on special that night, using my momma's secret recipe—and that may very well have been a part of it, but that wasn't all. Geraldine Pritchett was in my diner; that's what was drawing some of the crowd. Not just Geraldine, of course, but Naomi and Beth, too, along with Marissa. That's pretty big happenings, for Cedar Hollow. Truth is, I don't recollect Geraldine ever setting foot in the diner before, not even when we was girls. I don't imagine she was allowed to back then, and Geraldine had become something of a recluse after falling in with Junior. Anyhow, add the fact that she was there with the girls who'd run away from her nigh thirty years ago, and the curious will come out of the woodwork.

What was happening in Cedar Hollow might not have made *World News with Diane Sawyer*, but it was news, nonetheless, and I'd wager as important in its own way as anything else Ms. Sawyer was reporting on. After all, ain't it family that's supposed to be the foundation of this country? The Pritchetts in my diner that evening was looking like a mighty fine family indeed. That might have been the first time a statement like that was ever thought about the Pritchetts, but I don't think it'll be the last.

I don't know what they'd said to each other up in the boarding home, but I do know Naomi and Marissa showed up back in town with Beth a couple of hours after I'd sent them off to the creek. Didn't nobody see hide nor hair of them again until later in the afternoon when Darryl Lane saw Beth and Marissa walking out toward the creek again by themselves. I reckon it was another couple of hours before Virgil Young spotted them headed back to the boarding home, where Erma Puckett said they'd all holed up in Geraldine's room for the rest of the afternoon. I imagine Erma knew more about what was going on than she was saying, but I respected her for keeping it to herself; that was only right.

Whatever it was they'd said to each other, it appeared to have done a world of good for all of them. I was standing there, caught up in watching them instead of taking orders like I should have been doing, when Andrew surprised me with a kiss on top of my head. "You did good, Mom," he said with a smile, before going back to the grill.

When for generations your family has owned the only diner within fifty miles of town, you know things. I hadn't known how it would turn out, me calling those girls back home, but I figured I'd be hard pressed to make it any worse than it already was. Some people, like me, are blessed with a good family all the way around. Others, like Jessie, have the bad luck of being born into a mess that's better off left behind. But every now and then, a family comes along that shows a spark of hope in spite of the muddle they create for themselves. Geraldine and her girls, they had that spark. All I had to do was light it so they could find their way.

Book Club Discussion Starters

1. People from town whispered that Geraldine Pritchett was crazy, but she says, "I have outlived and outlasted anyone or anything I ever cared about, and I am finished. ... Tell me this: When a person is done living, what's crazy about dying?" What do you think? Was Geraldine crazy? Did she have a point?

2. Naomi describes what set the Pritchetts apart: "Our neighbors were impoverished and dignified; we were trash, and proud of it." What led Naomi to that conclusion? Is it accurate?

3. About her mother, Beth states, "... passivity was her sin." Do you agree? Which would you consider to be worse for the Pritchett children: a father who was physically abusive, or a mother who was passive and disconnected?

4. Kay Langley says, "It was just one of them situations where everybody is sort of right and everybody is sort of wrong all at the same time." Do you agree? Were there any members of Geraldine and Junior's family who weren't guilty in some way?

5. Geraldine says the first time she met Junior, "He looked right at me then and smiled a slow, wicked smile, and I felt a pull that never did let me go." Beth describes her mother as being "addicted" to her father. Do you agree? Can someone be addicted to another person?

6. Mark Sloan said, "Sometimes it made me angry that as Beth slowly lost sight of who she was, she lost sight of who I am as well." What did he mean by that? Do you think he was right?

7. Beth says, "I was not the sort of person to step in, placing myself front and center, to protect one of my siblings as Luke and Naomi often did." She states she was not as funny or talented as her siblings, and "... my need for self-preservation outranked my need to protect those whose ability to self-protect was stronger than my own." Was Beth cowardly for taking that stand?

8. Beth also says, "There was a stark honesty about our relationship with our father that wasn't present with my mother." What does she mean by this? Do you agree?

9. When discussing Luke's death, Beth says about her parents, "They set in motion a chain of events that killed him just as surely as I had." Do you agree? Who bears responsibility for Luke's death?

10. Kay Langley says, "Some people, like me, are blessed with a good family all the way around. Others, like Jessie, have the bad luck of being born into a mess that's better off left behind. But every now and then, a family comes along that shows a spark of hope in spite of the muddle they've created for themselves." Do you agree with Kay's assessment?

More Great Books by
Melinda Clayton

Appalachian Justice, Cedar Hollow Series, Book 1

Return to Crutcher Mountain, Cedar Hollow Series, Book 2

Shadow Days, Cedar Hollow Series, Book 4

Blessed Are the Wholly Broken

Making Amends

About the Author

Melinda Clayton is the author of *Appalachian Justice, Return to Crutcher Mountain, Entangled Thorns, Shadow Days, Blessed Are the Wholly Broken,* and *Making Amends.* In addition to writing, Dr. Clayton has an Ed.D. in Education Administration and is a licensed psychotherapist in the states of Florida and Colorado.